Dear Karen,

Happy Christmas,

Love

Peggy

(Margaret O'Neill)

Imogen's eyes met his.

After a moment Daniel said huskily, 'I'm glad that your loaded trolley was lying.'

'Lying?' Her voice was little more than a murmur.

'Yes.' He half smiled. 'All those groceries. I thought you were the mother of a whacking big family. I imagined you slaving over a hot stove all day and an ironing-board all night. Instead of which I find that you're a kind of Girl Friday helping out one of my favourite patients.' His smile broadened and he released her hand. 'I'm quite relieved.'

Margaret O'Neill started scribbling at four and began nursing at twenty. She contracted TB and, when recovered, did her British Tuberculosis Association nursing training before general training at the Royal Portsmouth Hospital. She married, had two children, and with her late husband she owned and managed several nursing homes. Now retired and living in Sussex, she still has many nursing contacts. Her husband would have been delighted to see her books in print.

Recent titles by the same author:

DOWNLAND CLINIC
NO LONGER A STRANGER
TAKE A DEEP BREATH
LONG HOT SUMMER
NEVER PAST LOVING
CHRISTMAS IS FOREVER

THE GENEROUS HEART

BY

MARGARET O'NEILL

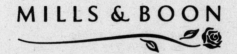

MILLS & BOON

MILLS & BOON, the Rose Device and
LOVE ON CALL are trademarks of the publisher.
Harlequin Mills & Boon Limited,
Eton House, 18-24 Paradise Road, Richmond, Surrey TW9 1SR
This edition published by arrangement with Harlequin Enterprises B.V.

© Margaret O'Neill 1995

ISBN 0 263 14586 7

Set in Times 10 on 11½ pt. by
Rowland Phototypesetting Limited
Bury St Edmunds, Suffolk

15-9510-48834

Made and printed in Great Britain
Cover illustration by Alexis Liosatos

CHAPTER ONE

IMOGEN was quite exhausted by the time she had finished doing the shopping. Her supermarket trolley was piled high. It was unbelievable that three adults and two children could consume so much, and even now she had the feeling that she had missed something basic and necessary from her list. It was almost as bad as a heavy day on the ward, she thought wryly. Oh, well, she decided philosophically, if it's anything important that I've forgotten, Laurie will just have to make an effort and fetch it later. Anyway, if he hadn't run out of practically everything in the house I wouldn't have had such a load to get.

A little spurt of annoyance shot through her as she took her place in what seemed to be the shortest queue at the check-out. Laurie really was the limit when it came to shopping or anything on the domestic front. He seemed to expect to be waited on hand and foot, although in other ways he was as thoughtful and charming as she remembered him in the past—if, unsurprisingly, rather more serious these days. No wonder Aunt Sophie had needed her help when she had fallen ill, for her son might be a talented business-man but he certainly couldn't cope with her, his children and his mother's busy little craft-cum-bookshop—especially now that the multi-national company he worked for was engaged in setting up regional offices, which often entailed his being away from home at irregular intervals.

Imogen resigned herself to a long wait behind several

well-stocked trolleys, and let her mind continue to wander over the last few hectic days.

She had called Aunt Sophie as soon as she had realised how ill she had become to ask if she could help in some way. Characteristically, the old lady had been hesitant about accepting the offer, and had made light of her condition. But Imogen, reading between the lines, had insisted. Eventually Aunt Sophie had agreed. 'That is,' she had said, 'if you can take some time off without too much inconvenience for a few weeks. . .then I'd be most grateful, Imogen. Things are a bit difficult at the moment, with the children distressed at being parted from their mother, and Laurie near the end of his tether. We could do with some support. You do understand that you would be more than my nurse—we need a sort of general factotum to help in the shop and with the children when Laurie's not here. . .?' She had hesitated. 'And you do realise we cannot afford to pay you as much as you will undoubtedly deserve? Laurie earns a good salary, but he's saving for a house and sending money back to America to his wife, and my income from the shop is adequate, but not magnificent. I'm not sure what the proper rate would be——'

'As long as I have board and lodging, I'll manage,' Imogen had said quickly, remembering only too well what a tower of strength Aunt Sophie had been to her when her parents had divorced and left her, a vulnerable teenager, devastated. She had comforted her and provided her with a home until matters between her parents had been sorted out, and she herself had started her nursing training.

Working hard at Bromfield General, her large northern teaching hospital, as well as visiting her separated parents, had meant that she had seen less of her aunt over recent years, but that hadn't broken the strong bond of affection that existed between them. Neither had it diminished her admiration for that wonderful woman, and, though she had only visited it a few times, Imogen still thought of the rambling Regency house in the small market town of Steynhurst, lying in a fold in the South Downs, as a second home.

It was just bad luck that Aunt Sophie's problems had come at the time when she was expecting promotion from staff nurse to junior ward sister. The SNO had been rather brisk about it, and said in no uncertain words that Imogen should wait at least until after her interview to go to her aunt's help.

'But she needs me now,' Imogen had said. 'Of course, she has no idea about this interview. She's a wonderful person, used to coping with her severe arthritis and a little craft-cum-bookshop that she owns. Recently she's had to accommodate her son, who has just come back from America, and his two children. But she herself needs nursing at the moment, because she's picked up a virus which has affected her mobility. I don't want to miss my interview, but I simply have to go and do what I can, Miss Fairly, so I'm applying for leave of absence.'

The record of events passed through her mind as she waited for the queue to move. She recalled now that she had spoken in a firm, calm voice, though she had been feeling desperately miserable at missing this opportunity to step up the nursing ladder. She had also been unable to explain the depth of her feelings for Aunt Sophie and the magnitude of the debt that she felt she owed her.

The SNO had shaken her head and looked at her as if she was mad. 'Well, I admire your sense of loyalty to your godmother, Staff Nurse, but how are you going to manage financially—this is unpaid leave you are asking for?'

'Well, I'll be getting board and lodging, plus something towards my time. . . My aunt insisted on that and I didn't want to offend her.'

'Couldn't she get in an agency nurse?'

'No, it's not just a nurse she needs, but someone who loves and cares for her and the family, and can help in the shop.'

'Well, do remember, Staff, that until you resign or are dismissed you are still legally employed by the local authority here, and any money that your godmother gives you must be in the form of a gift, not a fee or salary. And you do realise, don't you,' the SNO had said severely, 'that it might be a long time before you get the chance of promotion again? I can only keep your job open for a limited period.'

'Yes, I do, but I must go,' Imogen had said stubbornly. . .

'And I don't regret it,' she muttered fiercely to herself as she shoved her laden trolley forward when the queue began to move on at a snail's pace.

Her trolley met something hard and unyielding, and she realised that she had bumped into the person in front of her. 'Oh, I'm so sorry,' she said contritely as the man turned round to look at her. 'I do apologise.' She found herself looking up into a rugged, smiling face and a pair of twinkling hazel-green eyes.

'Think nothing of it,' the man said in a deep, warm voice. He raised a dark quizzical eyebrow. 'I hardly felt a thing.'

That's probably true, thought Imogen, taking in his height and his broad-shouldered, solid-looking frame. For some reason she felt that she ought to explain why she had bumped into him. 'I'm afraid I was daydreaming and didn't realise that I was so close to you. I wasn't being impatient.'

'Who could blame you if you were?' he said, looking with interest at her pile of groceries. 'You're obviously a very busy lady. But take heart, we're nearly there.' He gave another of his engaging smiles, and turned back to his own trolley as the queue started to move again.

It wasn't until he was unloading at the check-out that Imogen was able to see his purchases. They came as something of a surprise, for, instead of the mixed packages of food and fruit that she'd expected, his trolley was loaded with disposable nappies, baby lotion and powder.

Imogen gave an involuntary gasp, and the dark-haired man looked at her, a half-smile on his wide mouth. 'Big family,' he said cheerfully, obviously having interpreted her surprise. 'And infants go through an incredible number of these.' He pointed with a long finger at the nappies.

Imogen found herself apologising yet again. 'Sorry,' she said. 'That was rude of me.' She felt herself blushing.

'Not at all,' grinned the man. 'I'm used to it. I'm not bothered.' He moved down the counter to start loading his trolley at the other end, and Imogen automatically put the 'Next Customer' sign in place and started unloading her own goods.

The man paid for his purchases, exchanged some bantering chat with the check-out girl, who seemed to know him, and made for the exit.

Used to shopping for one, Imogen found the experience of bagging up her many purchases as they came off the check-out conveyor belt a totally new experience. She was conscious all the time of the people queuing behind her, and found herself rushing to put her things into the bags. However do women with several small children in tow manage? she thought, her estimation of them rising immeasurably.

At last she was finished and thankfully paid her bill and made for the car park; it had been very full when she had arrived, and her car was some way from the building. It had started to rain; icy winter rain, lancing down from a leaden sky and blown almost horizontal by the strong wind. She zipped up her weatherproof jacket, pulled on her warm gloves and raced for her car, a small hatchback dwarfed by a chunky Range Rover parked beside it. Through the driving rain she could just see the man who had stood in front of her in the queue unloading the last of his shopping into the back of the bigger vehicle.

He finished stowing his goods and moved across the small space between the cars. 'Here, let me give you a hand—it'll take you an age packing away that lot; you'll get soaked.'

Almost on the point of refusing help from this near-stranger, Imogen instead found herself stumbling out a thank-you, and allowing him to lift packages from the trolley into the boot of her car. His strong, capable hands made short work of the job. He seemed unaffected by the pouring rain, though his dark hair was sleeked down and water was running down between his neck and the upturned collar of his white, military-looking raincoat.

Imogen felt quite guilty that she'd allowed him to help her. 'Now you're soaked too,' she said, trying to blink the raindrops out of her blue eyes and running her fingers through her chestnut bob of hair. She felt her fringe plastered to her forehead and water trickling from it straight into her eyes.

'You look wetter,' he said, pulling a large folded handkerchief from his pocket. 'Allow me.' To her utter surprise, he leaned across the trolley, patted at her fringe and mopped gently round her eyes. 'What a blessing you're not wearing mascara,' he added matter-of-factly. 'That would be messy. Now, I'll take the trolleys back while you get home to your family.' He didn't give her a chance to answer, but raised a hand, and moved off, pushing the trolleys to the nearest bay.

'Thank you,' Imogen called after him. 'You've been very kind.' She wished that she could have explained that she didn't have a family. At least, not the sort that he obviously thought she had.

He raised his hand again in acknowledgement, but didn't look back. She felt a pang of regret that he hadn't turned to give her another of his nice smiles. She got into the driving seat of the car and drove slowly off, her mind full of the large, rugged stranger who had been so kind. A knight in a white raincoat. She giggled out loud. What a pity he's married—and heavily married, by the look of it, whispered a voice in the back of her head. The idea surprised her. She squashed the voice and concentrated on driving home through the downpour, which reduced visibility dramatically.

Once back from the outskirts to the middle of Steynhurst, she parked in the small space in front of the garage beside the shop, which fronted on to the High Street, and prepared to unload. The nearest way to get to the living quarters was through the shop, and, although the side-door was normally used to get to the private part of the house, Imogen felt that on this occasion she had a right to use the shorter route. She hauled out two heavy bags and let herself in through the shop door.

There were three people there, browsing among the books. Laurie came out from behind the counter.

'Imogen, you can't come in this way,' he hissed. 'Go round by the side-door.'

'What, in this weather? You've got to be joking. Here, take these. . .I'm going back for the other stuff.' She thrust the bags into Laurie's unwilling hands. 'Go on,' she said. She jerked her head towards the customers. 'They won't mind—they're only browsing.'

Laurie frowned at her, but took the bags and made for the door at the back of the shop. Though he was in sole charge of the shop only infrequently now, he disliked any disturbance in its routine. Perhaps he was compensating for the disorder and confusion that had recently plagued the rest of his life, Imogen thought charitably as she dived back outside into the pouring rain and collected more bags. It needed two further trips before the boot was empty. When she was finally done she discovered that Laurie hadn't moved any of the bags she had thrust inside the shop door, but was involved in a conversation with one of the customers. Surely he could have dragged himself away from the customer to give a hand? she thought savagely.

Snorting with disgust and anger, she carried the groceries through to the large family kitchen. 'My knight in a white mackintosh wouldn't have left me to do all the work,' she ground out to Bess the cat, curled up and fast asleep by the Aga. She stroked the elderly black and white creature, but Bess just twitched and slept on.

Before going out she had put a casserole in the slow oven for lunch, and this was steaming away aromatically. After she had packed the groceries away, Imogen made coffee for herself and Aunt Sophie, and took both mugs upstairs to the sitting-room.

Her aunt was sitting in the armchair where she had left her after helping her bath and dress earlier that morning. She looked terribly frail, but elegant and well groomed, having applied her make-up and perfume after Imogen had gone shopping.

'You poor darling,' said Aunt Sophie. 'I saw you from the window struggling in with the groceries. I thought that Laurie would have helped you.'

'There were customers in the shop,' said Imogen, automatically defending Laurie, both for his sake and her aunt's sensitive feelings.

'Really,' said Aunt Sophie. 'I'm sure that he could have spared a moment. The trouble is, he seems to think that domestic chores are beneath him, though where he got this idea from I don't know. It seems to have happened to him since he went to America.' She added almost apologetically, 'Perhaps his wife had rigid views about what she saw as her domain; I believe some women are like that.'

Imogen didn't reply—she had no answer to this argument. She thought that Laurie was behaving like a typical male chauvinist and could easily have bestirred himself some more, but she wouldn't dream of saying so to her aunt. Aunt Sophie's words made her think yet again of the man who had helped her at the supermarket. He had looked autocratic and rather chauvinistic himself on account of his masculine bearing and rugged features, and yet he had been only too ready to help, and had not minded shopping for the most basic things for his family. But then, he had seemed very confident and sure of himself, as if he didn't need to protect his image.

Oddly, a little wave of regret swept over her when she realised that she would probably never see him again. How could one feel like that, she asked herself, when you'd only just met someone and knew nothing about them? And yet she felt that there was a void in her life, a hollow feeling inside her. Why on earth had he made such an impact? She had absolutely no idea, only that it was a fact. Weird!

Her momentary sadness must have shown in her face, for Aunt Sophie put out an arthritic, distorted hand and patted hers. 'What's wrong, Imogen; why so sad? Is it going to be too much for you looking after me and my difficult family for a few weeks? If it is, then all you have to do is say so. . .'

Imogen was appalled to have shown her feelings so plainly. The last thing that she wanted to do was worry this dear old lady. Gently she massaged the crippled fingers that had deteriorated so rapidly recently. 'Of course it's not too much for me. I'm loving being here with you, and the twins need plenty of support at the moment; they must be missing their mother dreadfully.' She let go of Aunt Sophie's hands and stood up. 'Which reminds me that I'd better go down and relieve Laurie in the shop so that he can collect the children from school.' She dropped a light kiss on her godmother's pale cheek and made for the door.

Laurie came to meet her as she entered the shop, which was now empty. He held out both hands and took hers in his. 'Imogen,' he said in a subdued voice. 'I owe you an apology for my behaviour just now. It was unforgivable. You must have thought me all kinds of an inconsiderate swine.'

Imogen grinned. 'Because you didn't help me in with the shopping? Forget it, Laurie. I was mad at the time, but it's all over now. You were busy.'

He gave her an uncertain smile. 'I should have helped you.'

'Yes, you should,' she said with a shrug and a laugh.

'Next time you can come with me to the supermarket. That'll be your punishment.'

Laurie grimaced. 'It certainly would be a punishment,' he said with a laugh. 'But I'll do it.'

'Good. Now you'd better be off to fetch the children.'

'Yes, you're right.' He put a hand on her arm and said seriously, 'And Imogen, thank you for everything. We couldn't manage without you. I'm afraid that I've rather gone to pieces since Kim refused to come back with us from America. I've not been a lot of use to the kids, and certainly not to Mother, and my work being so erratic at the moment hasn't helped. But now you're here things might begin to look up a bit.' He leaned forward and kissed her in a friendly fashion on the cheek. 'Thanks again,' he said, and let himself out through the shop door.

Imogen was quite touched by his little speech. Perhaps she'd judged him too harshly. After all, he must have had a shock when his wife refused to come to England with him, and it must also have been pretty traumatic for him explaining to the twins, Patti and Jason. She gathered from the little that Aunt Sophie had said that there was another man involved, so having to come home, leaving the situation unresolved, had made it even worse for Laurie. And no wonder the children were either fractious and argumentative, or sullen and withdrawn. They had a new situation to contend with in an unfamiliar temporary home. Her heart went out to them and she resolved to be more loving and understanding, even if they seemed to go out of their way to annoy her. They had to take their frustrations out on somebody, and it was better that it was on her rather than their father or granny.

She went round the bookshelves tidying up the

books—half of them seemed to be out of alphabetical order. The old-fashioned shop bell rang as the door was opened. A browser probably, Imogen thought, unable to see the door and teetering, with a pile of books in her hands, on the little platform on top of the stepladder. 'I'll be with you in a moment,' she called. 'Please do look around.'

'Would that I could,' said a deep warm voice that she instantly recognised as belonging to the man in the queue at the supermarket. 'But I'm afraid my time is limited.'

Most of the books that she was holding slithered to the floor with a series of thumps. She found her voice. 'Oh,' she said. 'I'll come at once.' She started to climb down the ladder, her heart beating unaccountably unevenly, her mind in fast-forward. What was he doing here? If he hadn't much time, what was he looking for? Aunt Sophie's shop was definitely one that needed to be browsed in.

'Here, let me help you.' He was there at the foot of the ladder, hand held out ready to catch her or the books.

Imogen stepped down on to the floor and faced him.

He smiled, that lovely wide smile that had intrigued her earlier that morning. He didn't look particularly surprised at seeing her; he had the sort of face, she realised, that gave nothing away. 'So we meet again,' he said, and, to her astonishment, added, 'I somehow thought that we might.'

Caught off guard, Imogen said rather breathlessly, 'Well, I didn't.'

'Oh, really?' he said. 'I thought it was inevitable, though not in these surroundings.'

'Are you psychic or something?' She was recovering her calm.

'Not as far as I know,' he said cheerfully. 'It was just a feeling. If that's psychic, then that's what I am. I prefer to call it instinct.'

'That's a woman's prerogative, instinct.'

'No, they're better at it, that's all.'

Imogen pulled herself together; he was, after all, a customer. 'Anyway, psychic or not, what can I do for you, sir?'

'Well, nothing really—I've called to see Mrs Jackson.'

'I'm afraid she's not well. If it's something to do with the shop, perhaps I can help. Or Mrs Jackson's son can when he gets back—he won't be long.'

He grinned, and his hazel eyes twinkled. 'It's nothing to do with the shop. I'm not a rep or anything like that, I'm Dr Granger, Mrs Jackson's GP. . . Daniel Granger.' He held out a hand. 'And you are?'

Automatically Imogen put her hand into his and found the pressure of his fingers warm and oddly reassuring. She felt a tingling sensation up her arm. She swallowed, and said rather breathlessly, 'I'm Mrs Jackson's god-daughter and a sort of honorary niece, Imogen Moore. I'm helping out while she's ill.'

'A lovely name, Imogen.'

Her name rolled off his tongue in his deep, warm voice, giving it a richness that she hadn't heard before. She felt her cheeks flush.

She realised that her hand was still in his, and that the tingling sensation in her arm persisted. She made to withdraw her hand, but he increased the pressure of his fingers slightly, and she was trapped. She looked down at their clasped hands and then up into his face. The rain pelted against the window-panes, emphasising the quiet within the shop, empty except for the two of them.

Imogen lifted her head and her eyes met his. His eyes looked a darker green, less twinkly, rather serious, his well-shaped lips set in a firm line. After a moment he said huskily, 'I'm glad that your loaded trolley was lying.'

'Lying?' Her voice was little more than a murmur.

'Yes.' He half smiled. 'All those groceries. I thought you were the mother of a whacking big family. I imagined you slaving over a hot stove all day and an ironing-board all night. Instead of which I find that you're a kind of Girl Friday helping out one of my favourite patients.' His smile broadened and he released her hand. 'I'm quite relieved.'

'Relieved?' she asked as the shop doorbell clanged. They both looked at the door as an elderly couple entered accompanied by a gust of wind and a flurry of raindrops.

'Well, hello, Dr Granger,' called the woman. 'What a frightful morning.' The man, presumably her husband, nodded a greeting and made for the history section of the bookshelves.

'Terrible,' said Daniel to the woman, and then turned back to Imogen. 'It looks as if our conversation will have to wait,' he said softly. 'Another time perhaps. Now may I go up and see Mrs Jackson? I know the way.'

'Please do.' Imogen nodded and gestured to the door behind her marked 'Private'. She said stiffly, 'I'm sorry I can't leave the shop.'

'No matter, I'll explain to your aunt.' He went through the door and closed it quietly behind him.

All sorts of thoughts whirled round in her head. How had he been so sure that he would meet up with her again? Had he known that she was connected with Aunt Sophie and that he would see her when he visited? No, he'd been surprised to find her in the shop. He'd thought her a young mum with a large family. He'd said so, and had been pleased to find that she wasn't.

Her heart thumped uncomfortably. What had he meant by saying that he was relieved? It was almost as if. . . No, he couldn't mean that it gave him a chance to get to know her better; he wouldn't be so stupid. He was a married man and a doctor. Her heart plummeted. She had almost forgotten that in the excitement of meeting him again and experiencing his warm, long handshake. The man, doctor or not, was nothing but a philanderer, full of charm, but lethal. That white knight business was all a charade. He probably wouldn't have been half so kind had she been an elderly lady having problems with a laden trolley. No, that probably wasn't true. . .he seemed kind enough, but he must think her a fool to succumb to his charm.

A married man with a large family. Well! Who did he think she was to be swept off her feet by a sophisticated medical man—some kind of country bumpkin? Of course, he didn't know that she was from a large teaching hospital full of sophisticated medical men, some of whom thought that they were God's gift to the nursing fraternity and had to be regularly fought off.

At that moment the door behind her opened, though it wasn't the doctor but Laurie who stood there.

'I've got the children,' he said. 'Will you come and get them sorted for lunch while I take over here?'

'No,' said Imogen firmly, 'you see to your children and eat with them alone for a change. They need *your* company, Laurie, not mine. They should be with you as much as possible. I'll have my lunch later upstairs with Aunt Sophie.' Laurie gaped at her. 'And by the way, Dr Granger is with her. He'll probably want a word with you before he goes.'

'Oh,' Laurie said, slightly taken aback by her firmness. 'Well, if he wants a word with anyone it will be with you, as a nurse. He'll sort Mother out—he always does. They get on like a house on fire, even though she hasn't been on his list very long. Anyway, why won't you come and see to the twins?'

'Because you're quite capable of putting out their lunch, and they will appreciate having you to themselves. It's all ready in the oven; you only have to serve it.'

Laurie ran a hand through his short fair hair. 'OK,' he said. 'If you say so.'

Laurie really had to start facing up to his responsibilities, thought Imogen; both for his own sake and that of Jason and Patti. He was obviously highly capable within in his own specialised sphere of business management, but was quite lost when it came to some common-sense 'real world' matters. The image came again into her mind of Dr Granger, efficiently unloading his supermarket trolley, and even having time to chat with the check-out girl. They were certainly two very different men.

Over lunchtime the shop was quite busy, with nearby office workers coming in mostly to buy arty greetings cards and wrapping paper, and small handmade gifts for presents. Quite a number of them were regular customers who enquired after Aunt Sophie. It was quite heartwarming to find that she was held in such esteem.

It was while Imogen was talking to one of the regulars that Laurie appeared in the doorway behind her. 'The doctor wants to see you,' he said. 'He's in the office. It's something about an injection for Mother. I'll carry on here. The children have had their lunch. They liked your casserole, by the way—they actually said so.'

'Well, perhaps that's because you were alone with them. After all, after only three days I'm still almost a stranger. Now, I'd better go and see what Dr Granger wants.'

With some trepidation, following their rather strange meeting earlier, Imogen went through to the small room that Aunt Sophie used as an office. It was furnished with a desk, three chairs, a telephone and a filing cabinet.

Dr Granger was perched on the side of the desk writing on a prescription pad. He had removed his raincoat, revealing a beautifully cut, tweedy suit with a yellow waistcoat, absolutely right for a small country town doctor. He looked well groomed but casual.

He slid off the desk and looked down at her, dwarfing her not inconsiderable five feet seven. He was well over six feet tall, lean, broad shouldered, immensely fit looking, ruggedly handsome.

Impatiently Imogen suppressed the tremor of excitement that enveloped her as she looked at him. She must put all that nonsense behind her. She'd only met the man today, he was married and he shouldn't arouse any such feelings. She drew herself up to her full height.

'You wanted to see me,' she said in a steady voice, 'about Aunt Sophie.'

'Yes. I didn't know that you were a registered nurse.'

Imogen shrugged. 'Why should you? Your famous instinct was obviously not functioning as well as you thought when we met.'

The doctor laughed. 'You're dead right,' he replied.

'I must admit that it's a bit unreliable.'

'Well, what did you want, Doctor? Laurie said something about an injection?'

He looked at her severe expression, frowned, and dropped his bantering attitude. 'That's right,' he said seriously. 'I did some blood tests on Mrs Jackson last week and I've just got the results back. She's anaemic and I want to start her on a course of iron by deep intramuscular injection. I could ask the community nurse to call, but, as you're here in the role of private nurse to your aunt, I thought you would rather treat her yourself.'

'Yes, of course; I'm only too pleased to do what I can. I wish more could be done to help the pain and the stiffness in her joints, though. She's certainly deteriorated since that virus attack.'

'That's true. I alternate her various pain-killers and anti-inflammatory agents to try to keep it under control, but without much success, I'm afraid. I'd like her to have physiotherapy, but for some reason she's against it. Perhaps you could persuade her to give it a go; it might just help.'

'Of course; I'll do what I can.' She took the prescription that he offered her. 'When do you want me to start this?'

'Tomorrow, please. Perhaps you or Mr Jackson could collect it from the chemist today?'

'Yes, will do. Is that all?'

He looked at her face, which was stiff with determination not to give in to his charm, and said softly, 'Yes, for the moment just carry on doing what you can for your aunt. She appreciates your being here very much, and I'm sure that her son and the children are glad to have you around. Although, as I understand from Mrs Jackson, the children are rather difficult to handle at the moment. You've certainly got your work cut out, looking after a distressed family and a sick, elderly lady, but I'm sure you'll cope—you're the coping sort.' He gave her a wide, friendly, reassuring smile, and his hazel eyes twinkled.

She felt absurdly pleased by the small compliment, and found herself smiling back. Whatever his faults, he really was a kind man and a good doctor. 'Yes, I'll cope,' she said firmly. 'Aunt Sophie's a great fighter, and the children will hopefully soon bounce back.'

'Children have a habit of doing that against all the odds. They're natural fighters—just as you are. But if I might venture a word of advice, don't be too soft in your dealings with them all the time, as you might be tempted to be because you feel sorry for them, or they'll run rings round you. They'll respect you for it if you're occasionally a little tough, make a few rules. Children like to know where they stand; they feel safe.' He smiled wryly. 'Sorry, that was impertinent of me, attempting to advise you. I'm sure you know all this.'

His eyes met hers, and for a moment the same little thrill of magic swept over her as it had earlier in the shop. She squashed the feeling, refusing to be charmed. It was ridiculous. She said woodenly, 'Well, Doctor, if that's all, I must give Aunt Sophie her lunch, and I'm sure you're a busy man and want to get back to the surgery. . .or home.'

He grimaced. 'Would that I could, but I've several more calls to make yet.' He looked at her calm, unsmiling face. 'Goodbye,' he said abruptly, turning towards the door. 'I'll call again next week, but get in touch if you need me before then. I'll see myself out.'

He was gone, closing the door quietly behind him.

For a few minutes Imogen stared at the closed door, then sighed heavily, pinned a smile on her face, and went upstairs to attend to her aunt.

CHAPTER TWO

IMOGEN found the next few days wearing, to say the least. She seemed to be making no progress in building up a relationship with the twins, who appeared to resent her more daily.

She tried to be infinitely patient, but matters came to a head three mornings after her meeting with Dr Granger, when he had so confidently predicted that she would *cope* and that the twins would bounce back.

It was eight o'clock, and she and Laurie and the children were seated at the long refectory table in the comfortable old-fashioned kitchen, fragrant with coffee and toast. It should have been a nice family occasion, but the twins were being particularly truculent that morning. Their large grey eyes surveyed Imogen stonily across the table.

'Yuck, I don't want *that*,' said Patti rudely, pushing away her plate as Imogen placed it in front of her.

Holding on to her temper, Imogen said quietly, 'But you asked for scrambled eggs, Patti, and that's what you've got.'

'They're not done like my mom used to do them. I don't want them.' Patti tossed her head and her short fair plaits bounced defiantly. 'I want an up-and-over egg.'

'And so do I,' said Jason, following Patti's lead as he usually did and pushing his plate jerkily back across the table.

Imogen looked towards Laurie, who was buried behind the *Financial Times*, but he seemed not to have noticed—or was refusing to notice what was going on—for he didn't look up. Clearly she wasn't going to get any support from him.

For a moment Imogen was tempted to play along with the children, remove their untouched plates and cook them up-and-over eggs as they demanded. Then common sense prevailed. She mustn't give in to them as she had been doing over the last few days in order to win their confidence or affection. That hadn't worked; in fact, they almost seemed to despise her for it. She must be firm.

Their father might be too despondent or too indifferent to care how they behaved, but she wasn't, and Aunt Sophie, their grandmother, certainly wouldn't expect her to tolerate such bad behaviour. There was a limit as to how much they should be allowed to get away with because of the trauma of the break-up between their parents. She might want to be over-indulgent because of their distress, but it wasn't necessarily right to smother them with love and sympathy.

What had Dr Granger said? 'They'll respect you for it if you're occasionally a little tough. Children like to know where they stand; they feel safe.'

It wasn't going to be easy, being tough, but she knew she had to try. She took a deep breath, looked first at Patti and then at Jason, and said evenly, 'Oh, well, please don't eat them if you don't want to, but I'm not doing any more cooking this morning—I've plenty of other things to do.' She gave them a bright smile. 'You can always make up with toast and marmalade; it won't hurt you for once not to have a cooked breakfast.'

Patti glared at her, her eyes moist. She blinked. 'But Mom says that we always have to have a cooked breakfast before we go to school, it's important.' She looked towards her father. 'Daddy, make Imogen give us up-and-over eggs.'

With obvious reluctance, Laurie lowered his paper. 'But I can't *make* Imogen do anything, poppet. She's here looking after us because she wants to, not because she has to.'

'Well, I wish she wasn't here.' Violently Patti pushed back her chair, scraping it noisily over the tiled floor. 'I hate her and I want my mom,' she said, and stood up and burst into tears.

Jason's lip quivered. He stood up and sidled up to his sister. 'And I want my mom too.' He looked at his father and then at Imogen, and silent tears began to trickle down his cheeks.

Laurie sat immobile, staring at his two children helplessly.

Imogen said through clenched teeth, 'Laurie, do something. . .cuddle them.'

He said huskily, 'Oh, my God, I can't. This is too much,' and buried his face in his hands.

Slowly Imogen stood up, moved round the table and stood between the two children. She put her arms about them and hugged them close. They needed comforting, and she was the only one who could do it.

She thought that they would push her away, but, surprisingly, they didn't. They clung to her and sobbed as though their hearts would break.

Imogen let them cry, dropping kisses on their bent fair heads and murmuring endearments. A good cry never hurt anyone, as Aunt Sophie would say. And anything was better than the sullen silence they had maintained over the last week or so.

Eventually their sobs subsided, and Patti, blowing her nose on her sodden handkerchief, lifted a tear-stained face to Imogen's. She said in a wobbly voice, 'I didn't mean that about hating you, I just, just. . .'

'Hate the world for what's happened,' said Imogen softly. 'I know, love. That's how I felt when my parents split up.'

'I didn't know that had happened to you.'

'I'll tell you about it some time, but not now—you've got to get ready for school.'

'Can't we stay home today?' Jason asked wistfully. 'I feel funny.'

'You'll have to ask your father that,' Imogen said firmly, 'but if I were you, I'd be brave and go. You'll feel better if you keep busy—isn't that right, Laurie?' She looked at him over the children's heads, hoping that he would pull himself together. He owed that at least to the children.

He raised a ravaged-looking face but managed a tight smile. 'Imogen's quite right,' he said. 'But then, she usually is, bossy boots. It's better that we all keep busy.' He stood up and walked over to them and held out his arms. 'Come on, kids, let your useless old daddy give you a great big hug, and let's all try to be brave.'

Imogen pushed the children gently towards him, and crept quietly out of the kitchen.

A little later, having seen the children off to school, subdued but rather happier than usual, she went upstairs to attend to Aunt Sophie. As she helped her shower and dress, and administered her iron injection, she gave a potted version of what had happened that morning at breakfast, omitting Laurie's dismal behaviour.

Aunt Sophie said softly, 'So that's why the twins were much more amenable this morning. I'm so glad; it was lovely seeing them behaving like normal children. I wondered what had happened, as they were so much less sullen, much more affectionate. A good cry obviously did them good—they needed to get all that resentment out of their systems. Well done, Imogen. It obviously paid dividends deciding not to give in to them.'

Incurably honest, Imogen explained. 'I can't really take credit for that; it was Dr Granger who suggested a firm hand, and it worked.'

Her godmother nodded. 'I'm not surprised; Daniel Granger is a very thoughtful and intelligent young man. And he has the right attitude, that of the old-fashioned GP; he wants to *know* his patients in the round, their background, not just their medical history. He's a thoroughly splendid doctor and a real gentleman.'

Imogen didn't feel too sure about the real gentleman bit. Would he, a married man, have made passes at her if he was? 'Does he live here in Steynhurst?' she asked casually, trying not to sound too interested.

'Oh, yes, he bought Dr Robinson's old house fairly recently, next to the new health centre. Very convenient.'

'Yes, very,' replied Imogen. And a large old house, she thought drily, just right for the doctor's large family. A pang of regret went through her that such a good doctor who'd earned her aunt's respect should indulge in even a mild flirtation with her, and on such a brief acquaintance. Or was she over-reacting to his manner? Would she be so condemnatory of some other man? Was it because under any other circumstances she could have been attracted to a man like him? Who are you kidding? said an inner voice. You *are* attracted to the man.

Aunt Sophie was in a talkative mood. She continued,

'Of course, he's so busy at the moment, just having come back from holiday, with one of the partners off sick. He's not been able to get on with the alterations that he wants to make to his new home. Old Dr Robinson let the house go to pieces after his wife died, so there's a lot of decorating to do, and several of the rooms are apparently damp and unusable, so he was telling me. And at the moment he's got his people with him, so he's really got his hands full.'

'His people?' asked Imogen.

'His parents. His father has just retired from general practice in London. He and his wife are waiting to move into a bungalow on the coast, but there's been a hitch of some sort and they're staying with our Dr Granger while it's sorted out.'

'Oh, it must be a bit crowded,' said Imogen, thinking of Daniel's family as well as his parents occupying Dr Robinson's shabby old house, even thought it was a good size.

Aunt Sophie looked surprised. 'Not really,' she said. 'There's plenty of room for the three of them, even with some of the rooms out of use.'

The three of them? Imogen, who had been massaging her aunt's swollen feet and legs with oil before putting on her stockings, sat back on her heels and looked at her in surprise. 'But what about. . .?' she started to say, when there was a knock at the bedroom door.

'Come in,' called Aunt Sophie, and Pam Frost, her help, who had been with her for years, opened the door.

'I don't want to be a nuisance,' she said, 'but I've cut myself rather badly with the bread knife and I thought that Imogen might put a bandage on for me.' She was holding a towel round her left hand.

Imogen sprang up. 'Of course,' she said, 'let me look.'

Carefully she unwrapped the blood-soaked towel and exposed a long diagonal cut across the palm of Pam's hand which was bleeding copiously. She reformed the towel into a pad, pushed Pam on to a chair and held the arm upwards, pressing the pad on the wound as she did so.

'You're going to need stitches,' she explained. 'I'll take you to the casualty unit at the hospital in Fordham.'

'No, don't do that,' said Pam. 'They're handling small injuries at the health centre now. I don't want to go to the hospital because it'll take hours.'

Imogen looked doubtful.

Aunt Sophie confirmed this. 'We were all sent letters,' she said, 'saying that this was one of the new services they were providing for their patients.'

'Right, I'll phone and see what they say. Now, Pam, keep your arm up, and keep pressing the pad. May I?' she asked her aunt, picking up her cordless phone.

Aunt Sophie nodded. 'Be my guest,' she said. 'Just get Pam help as soon as possible.'

Imogen got through to the health centre. 'If she's a patient here, bring her straight along,' said the receptionist. 'The duty doctor will see her.'

When they arrived the receptionist handed them over to the duty sister, who took them through to a small but well-equipped surgery. She looked at the gaping wound, and replaced the makeshift blood-stained towelling pad with a sterile one that she fixed in place with strapping. She asked Imogen to apply pressure while she asked Pam some questions and filled in forms.

'You'll be pleased to know,' she said, 'that Dr

Granger, your own doctor, is on emergency duty today, and he'll be here to look at you shortly.'

A few minutes later Daniel strode into the room. Imogen was surprised and annoyed by her reaction to him. She felt herself blushing and was aware that her heart was beating fast and unevenly as she looked at him. Ludicrous.

'Hello, Mrs Frost,' he greeted Pam. 'What have you been up to?'

'I cut myself with a bread knife, Doctor, while I was working in Mrs Jackson's kitchen. Never done such a daft thing before. I wasn't concentrating, I was day-dreaming.'

Daniel's hazel eyes switched from Pam's face to Imogen's, and they were bright with humour. 'Ah, well,' he said, 'we all daydream at times, don't we, Miss Moore?' He was teasing her, of course, alluding to their first meeting in the supermarket when she had bumped into him with her piled-up trolley.

His hazel eyes twinkled, and she found herself giving him a warm smile. 'Yes,' she said, 'we do.'

He grinned widely, the creases on either side of his mouth deepening as he did so. He was a man who looked as if he smiled often, thought Imogen, though at the same time there was a steel-like quality, a reserve about him that belied the easy smile and the twinkling eyes. There was a depth to him that was not at first apparent, and perhaps it was this that his patients so readily responded to. Surely he couldn't be a light-weight philanderer, no matter what had passed between them?

Gently he took Pam's hand in his and removed the dressing. He examined the wound carefully. 'Well, Mrs Frost, it looks clean enough,' he said, 'but we'll wash it with an antiseptic before I stitch you up and dust it off with an antibiotic powder, and Sister will give you an anti-tetanus jab. Don't worry, it won't hurt; I'll numb your hand before I start embroidering, so you shouldn't feel anything.'

The sister cleaned the wound and Dr Granger sprayed Pam's hand with an anaesthetising agent, and left it for a few moments to work before commencing stitching.

Imogen admired his quick, neat work, and the way that he gave Pam an occasional reassuring smile. She was very impressed. He really is a good doctor, she thought, and wondered yet again if she'd imagined his personal, over-friendly approach to her. She just couldn't believe that a doctor as good as he was, with his personal commitments, would indulge in even a mild flirtation. Maybe he was separated or even divorced from his wife and felt free to chat up any passable female? No, it couldn't be that. He'd mentioned his family to explain his trolleyful of nappies. If he was estranged from his wife he'd hardly be doing the family shop for such items. On the other hand, Aunt Sophie had implied that he was living in Cleeves, Dr Robinson's old house, with just his parents, so his own family definitely wasn't with him. It was a mystery—but one that she hoped to solve as soon as possible.

Suddenly Imogen realised that Daniel was addressing her. 'Sorry,' she mumbled, jerked out of her reverie. 'What did you say?'

'Daydreaming again?' he asked with a quirky smile and raised eyebrows.

'Er—not exactly, I—I just didn't hear you. I was admiring your stitching,' she said, which was at least partially true.

He looked faintly surprised. 'Thank you,' he said. 'I've been telling Mrs Frost that she should rest her hand for a day or so, give it a chance to heal, but she seems to think that your aunt's household will fall to pieces if she's not there. Perhaps you could reassure her.'

Imogen said quickly, 'Of course we'll miss you, Pam, but please take the rest of the week off—I'll cope with the house.'

'What, and help in the shop, and look after Mrs Jackson?'

'Yes, and Laurie's there to help too, don't forget, and Doreen's due back in the shop tomorrow, so I can see to the cooking and cleaning. It'll only be for a few days, Pam, and I know that Aunt Sophie would want you to rest your hand; she'll worry if you don't.'

'OK,' she agreed resignedly, 'I'll give it to the end of the week.'

Daniel prescribed some pain-killers for Pam to take when sensation began to return to her hand. He patted her shoulder. 'And don't worry,' he said. 'I'm sure Miss Moore is more than capable of looking after the shop and anything else that crops up. According to her aunt, she's a very able young woman, you know.' He gave Imogen a brilliant smile, and with a casual goodbye left the surgery to return to his office. Sister Carpenter administered the anti-tetanus injection, and a few minutes later they were free to leave the health centre.

'What a dreamboat,' sighed Pam as they drove down the busy High Street towards her home on the outskirts of the town. 'I wish I were a free woman and thirty years younger. . .I could go for him in a big way.'

'Who?' asked Imogen with pretended innocence.

Pam looked sideways at her in surprise. 'Why, Dr Granger, of course—he's smashing. Don't you fancy him? I thought you looked pleased to see him when he came into the surgery, and you both laughed together at some joke, as if you understood each other well. It was almost as if you were old friends.'

Imogen was shocked that she seemed to have given herself away, especially to someone as down to earth and practical as Pam, who was not a person given to fanciful perceptions. She shrugged. 'Well, we're not,' she said, sounding very cool and indifferent. 'We only met a few days ago. And he's all right, I suppose, though a bit too confident for my liking. But then, a lot of doctors are; it goes with the territory. It's probably what makes him good at his job, and his manner is certainly very reassuring. But I think I'm immune to doctors, having worked with so many over the years.'

There, she thought, that should squash any outlandish notions that Pam might have. The trouble was that it also made it impossible for her to ask Pam anything further about him.

But Pam was like a dog with a bone; she wouldn't leave go.

'Your aunt Sophie likes him a lot,' she persisted.

'Well, of course she does. As I said, he's a good doctor and a kind man. . .what more could a patient want? And how's your hand feeling?' she asked abruptly, changing the subject as she pulled up in front of Pam's house.

'It's throbbing a bit now it's coming back to life. That's why I've been nattering like mad, to keep my mind off it,' replied Pam. She looked hard at Imogen, whose face was rather set and serious, and said, sounding guilty, 'I didn't mean to say anything out of turn.' She looked apologetic.

'What on earth do you mean, out of turn?'

'Well, sort of suggesting that you and Dr Granger might. . .' She trailed off, clearly embarrassed. 'It was silly of me. It's not possible, of course, because I've heard that he's. . .' Again she broke off, and pulled a face. 'I'm sorry, Imogen, I was spouting nonsense. I should mind my own business.'

Imogen put on a carefree smile and tried to live up to her earlier show of indifference. 'Don't worry about it. He's an attractive man and people are bound to talk about him. I bet half the females in Steynhurst would fall over themselves to get him if he was available. I'm just not one of them, and he's not available.' She turned to her passenger, who was sitting looking rather pale, holding her left hand. 'Come on,' she said briskly. 'Let's get you indoors and I'll make you a cup of tea, which you can have with your pain-killers.'

Once inside the house, she settled Pam in an arm-chair with a cushion to rest her left arm on, and went through to the kitchen to make the tea.

While they were drinking their tea she suggested that Pam wear a sling to support her arm when moving about. 'A scarf will do,' she explained. 'Just enough to take the weight of your arm and remind you to go careful with it.'

'There's one in the drawer there,' said Pam. 'Will that do?'

Imogen fetched it. 'It's fine,' she said. 'Here, this is how you put it on.' She fixed the makeshift sling in place.

'That feels marvellous!' Pam exclaimed. 'Much more comfortable. Like your aunt says, you're a good nurse.'

At that moment they heard a key in the front door lock, and a moment later Tom Frost appeared.

He crossed the room and looked anxiously down at his wife. 'How are you, love?' he asked. 'Mrs Jackson rang me at work to tell me what had happened, so I've come home a bit early.'

'I'm all right. Imogen's made me comfortable and Dr Granger put some stitches in my hand. I've got to go back at the end of next week to have them out if they're ready.'

Imogen stood up and smiled at them both. 'I must be off,' she said, and turned to Tom. 'Don't let her do too much today; she's had a bit of a shock. Make sure that she takes her pain-killers and do let us know if there is anything else we can do.' She moved to the door. 'I'll let myself out, Tom—you stay with Pam.'

He nodded, and put his arm protectively round Pam's shoulders.

Pam said, 'Goodbye, Imogen; thanks for taking me to the surgery and making me comfortable. It was kind of you.'

'Not at all, it was the least I could do.' She waved a dismissive hand, and let herself out of the comfortable sitting-room, leaving them together.

Must be great, she thought as she started the car, to be married that long and care so much. Or perhaps I notice it because my parents didn't seem to care a bean about each other? In the end only Aunt Sophie really cared.

The thought occupied her during the short drive back home, that and the knowing suggestions that Pam had made about her reaction to the ruggedly handsome doctor. Had she been so obvious? And what had Pam meant when she had started to say that it wasn't possible—what wasn't possible? She had said that she'd heard something. . .what had she heard? Of course, since Dr Granger had not been that long in the district, his private life might still actually be just that—private. And yet Pam had somehow given the impression that he was not a married man, although he was not an entirely free agent. What on earth did that mean? Did it matter?

Yes, she admitted to herself, it does to me. I'm curious about the man. It's ridiculous when I barely know him, but he attracts me. I want to know more about him. I want to know why someone who seems to be such a devoted family man not ashamed to be seen buying nappies is not living with his family.

She was no nearer an answer to any of her queries when she arrived home. She found that Aunt Sophie had managed to struggle into her stockings and finish dressing, and with the aid of her walking frame had got herself to the sitting-room.

'How's Pam?' she wanted to know directly Imogen appeared.

Imogen filled her in on what had happened at the health centre, and gave her the cheering news that Pam would only be off till the end of the week.

'Oh, that's splendid news. But she mustn't rush back,' she said, then pulled a face. 'Though that's easy for me to say, useless as I am. It's going to mean more work for you with Pam away.'

'Don't worry, darling, I'll cope,' said Imogen, giving her aunt a hug. 'It'll be so much easier with the twins being happier and more settled. It'll be a piece of cake.'

'Well, hardly that,' said Aunt Sophie, 'but I know what you mean. And aren't we lucky,' she added, to Imogen's astonishment, 'to have Daniel Granger to look after us? He's such a splendid doctor. Young, but a good old-fashioned-type GP. He'll be a real support to us as a family.'

'Yes,' said Imogen, unable to think of anything else to say. 'I suppose he will.'

*   *   *

Imogen felt herself thinking about Daniel Granger a great deal over the next few days. Somehow she couldn't get him out of her mind. She should be able to put him out of her mind, but she couldn't, even though with Pam away she was busy in the house as well as looking after Aunt Sophie and the children. But no amount of housework, nursing or nannying could blot him quite out of her mind.

The fact was, she decided one morning, she was bored. She was missing full-time nursing, for what she had to do for Aunt Sophie was minimal after staffing on a busy ward. An occasional injection, helping her to bathe and dress, massaging the stiff joints and oedematous legs—that was the sum total of her nursing, and it wasn't enough.

She helped regularly in the shop, covering for Laurie when he went off every few days on business, and that was interesting enough. And that she was now getting on well with the twins was a great consolation, though clearly they missed their mother and were deeply confused by the present situation, and she was only a stopgap in whom they could confide, someone warm and loving. But even their increasing dependency on her couldn't fill the void. She was, she realised, busy and active but not as fully stretched and involved as hospital work had kept her. She would have to find something else to do to keep herself satisfactorily occupied.

This was further underlined when, at the beginning of the following week, Pam returned to work, her hand neatly bandaged and protected by a rubber glove.

'It's great to be back,' she told Imogen. 'I'm bored stiff at home.'

'I know the feeling,' replied Imogen drily. 'Only please don't tell Aunt Sophie. Her life revolves round the shop; mine is around nursing.'

'My lips are sealed,' replied Pam with a laugh.

A few days later Imogen heard from the hospital that her leave of absence would be suspended if she didn't return within the month, because her post had to be filled. She was advised to reapply for work when she was free to return to the hospital, although a placement wasn't guaranteed.

The news came as a shock to her, and she was glad that she was on her own in the kitchen having an after-breakfast cup of coffee when the letter arrived, giving her time to pull herself together and think over what she should do. Aunt Sophie was making progress, and should be much more active in a few weeks' time. Patti and Jason were beginning to settle in to their English home and school, and getting to know and love their grandmother. Laurie was still rather a lost soul, presumably pining for his wife, but he was due to start full-time work soon, when the regional offices were operating properly, which would give him a terrific boost. He liked routine, and Imogen hoped it would help stabilise his life. At least then he could justify getting a regular au pair for the children, and more help for his mother in the shop. One way or another it would be settled.

Or would it?

And where would that leave her? Was there any need for her to commit herself beyond the next three weeks?

She couldn't make up her mind. Aunt Sophie, she knew, depended on her for more than nursing and physical help, and so did the children and Laurie, though no way would her aunt seek more assistance, instead trying desperately to be independent. They all had emotional needs, and at the moment she was the best one to meet them. But what about when they ceased to need her, emotionally or otherwise? What if Laurie became totally involved with his job, and the children rightly became dependent on him and their grandmother, rather than on a sort of courtesy nanny? Where would that leave her? Above all, if Aunt Sophie made the sort of recovery that she might, and resumed daily life more or less normally, would she need her god-daughter around all the time? No, she decided, not really.

It was the timing that was difficult. Would three weeks be long enough for all those at present dependent upon her to rally? Supposing she went back to Bromfield, took up her old job as staff nurse, and left her aunt and the others at Steynhurst before they were ready? Her initial sacrifice of missing her promotion interview would be null and void, and she would have let Aunt Sophie down.

It was as she was wrestling mentally with the problem, painfully aware that her decision would affect her career for the next few years, if not longer, when there was a knock at the side-door of the house. She got up from the breakfast-table to answer it.

Daniel Granger stood on the doorstep.

'Hello,' he said cheerfully as soon as she opened the door. 'Sorry I'm a few days late coming to see Mrs Jackson, but I've been rather busy.'

Imogen felt her cheeks reddening at the sight of him, and her heart fluttering, but she kept her voice cool and businesslike. 'That's quite all right, Doctor, we guessed that you were fully occupied with your partner away, and Aunt Sophie is doing fine, so I didn't need to call you for anything.' She opened the door wide. 'Do come in,' she said.

Daniel stepped into the kitchen. 'Coffee smells gorgeous,' he said.

'Would you like a cup?' Imogen asked bluntly, rather ungraciously, still trying to hide her confusion.

'Love one, please.' Daniel ran his hand over his chin, dark with stubble. 'Been out on a couple of early calls,' he said. 'Haven't had time to breakfast or shave, but thought that I would visit here on my way to the surgery.' Lips curving at the corners, eyebrows raised quizzically, he gave her a quirky smile. 'I must look a sight,' he said.

'No, you don't,' replied Imogen quickly. 'You look. . .' Her voice faded. 'You look fine,' she said firmly, thinking that his designer-type stubble suited his rugged masculine looks. 'Just a touch short of your usually correct and immaculate image.' She smiled at him.

'You're having me on!' he exclaimed.

'No, just teasing a little,' she said gently, and added, 'You must be very tired!' There were crow's feet and dark smudges round his eyes.

'Nothing that a cup of your coffee and a good wash and brush-up won't put right,' he said briskly, returning her smile. 'Do you think that I might use a bathroom? I've got my battery razor with me; I just need a bit of time and space.'

'Feel free,' she said. 'There's a bathroom to the left at the top of the stairs.'

'Thanks. I'll take this with me if I may.' He indicated his mug of coffee, which she had thrust into his hand, and added wryly, 'One of the drawbacks of living next to the surgery is being on view to everyone in the waiting-room, and I'd rather they didn't see me this morning apparently skiving off home.' He shook his head. 'Some of them,' he said, 'will never believe that I've been out half the night on legitimate business.'

'I'll vouch for you,' Imogen said lightly.

'Right, many thanks.' Daniel lifted his mug of coffee. 'Now, if you don't mind, I'll go and make myself decent and then visit your aunt.'

'I'll let her know that you're coming.'

Daniel nodded and disappeared upstairs, and a few minutes later Imogen went up and explained to her aunt what was happening.

'Poor Daniel,' said Aunt Sophie, on hearing that he'd been out half the night. 'He must be exhausted. Do you think he'd like breakfast, Imogen?'

'I doubt it—he's anxious to get to the health centre. But he's had coffee. He won't starve, Aunt Sophie, and he'll survive till lunchtime.'

Imogen stayed with her aunt until Daniel, freshly shaven and looking his usual neat self, appeared to examine her.

It didn't take him long. Imogen had kept notes of her progress, which he accepted without hesitation.

'You're in good hands,' he told Aunt Sophie. 'Your god-daughter's an excellent nurse.'

'And wasted on me,' said Aunt Sophie, to Imogen's surprise. 'She copes with everything here so easily; she needs to have a more stimulating challenge. You can't suggest anything, Daniel, can you? I don't want to lose her. . .I don't want her to get restless.'

It was almost, Imogen thought, as if Aunt Sophie had read her mind and knew that she was bored without her nursing commitments. She said rather stiffly, 'Do you mind, what's all this "her" business? I am here, you know, in the room; I'm not a puppet.'

Aunt Sophie looked contrite. 'Sorry, Imogen, I wasn't thinking. You're quite capable of managing your own affairs and I mustn't interfere. I just thought that Daniel might. . .' Her voice trailed off.

'Might have an answer,' said Daniel. 'Well, you

know, I might at that.' He turned to Imogen. 'Could you come to the health centre after surgery tonight, say, about sevenish?' he asked. 'To have a word with me and some of my colleagues? You may be just the sort of person we are looking for to fill a gap in our service to our patients.'

Imogen stared at him in astonishment for a moment. 'Doing what?' she asked.

'Twilight nursing. Visiting patients in their homes between, say, five and ten in the evenings. We've been thinking about appointing somebody for some time.'

'But I've no experience of community nursing.'

Daniel shrugged. 'But you're a nurse, you can give injections, change dressings, etcetera, and you can work without supervision. That's obvious from the way you've cared for Mrs Jackson.' He gave her a nice friendly smile, and his eyes held hers for the fraction of a moment. 'And I'm sure that you're a kind, caring person, and that's what we need, to sort people out for the night, give them a sense of security, make them comfortable, especially if they have just come out of hospital. A very important job.'

Imogen felt a little thrill of excitement. The work sounded interesting and challenging, and the offer could hardly have come at a better time. Besides, it would give her a chance to see more of. . . She silently headed off that line of thought, and replied, in what she hoped was a suitably cautious manner, 'All right, I'll come and talk to you this evening. But that doesn't mean that I'm committing myself.'

'Fair enough. Just come along and have a chat.' He moved to the door. 'Bye now; I'll see myself out.' Quietly he closed the door behind him and went down the stairs.

Imogen realised that Aunt Sophie was subjecting her

to a kindly but penetrating gaze. 'You look even more pleased than I imagined you would, my dear,' she commented.

'Aunt Sophie, do you believe in fate?' Imogen asked brightly.

'Yes,' replied Aunt Sophie. 'As a matter of fact, I do.'

CHAPTER THREE

AFTER she had got over her initial burst of enthusiasm Imogen spent the rest of the day wondering if she had done the right thing by agreeing to go for a chat about the twilight nursing job. It wasn't that she doubted her own ability to cope with the nursing side of the work, but she did wonder how she would manage going into other people's homes. There was, she reflected, a big difference between that and hospital nursing, with all the back-up available, in spite of what Daniel had said about her managing easily. She was more than competent, and very caring, but apart from her experience with Aunt Sophie she was not used to working on her own.

There was too the added complication, as she saw it, that might arise if she had to work with Daniel. This morning he had seemed just casually and cheerfully friendly, and that had been fine, but supposing he got over-friendly again. . .how could she cope with that? She knew that she was attracted to him, but no way was she going to play 'the other woman' in some sort of triangle in his life, however he conducted his family affairs, which still remained shrouded in mystery.

Over the last few days she had got no further in learning the truth about him and his family. There were times when she thought that she never would without asking Aunt Sophie direct what his marital situation was, and where his family lived, but she was still reluctant to do this and reveal her interest in him.

It was a foolish situation, she knew, and partly a problem of her own making, but that made it no less real or inconvenient. Naturally straightforward by nature, she was coming to realise that occasionally it became impossible to ask the obvious question. Besides, she rationalised, surely I'll learn the facts about Daniel Granger eventually, simply by keeping my ears open. . .won't I?

The trouble was that he had apparently been in the area long enough for the inevitable early wave of gossip and fact-spreading about him to die down, but not long enough for all the details of his background to have become ingrained into the community.

Pam Frost seemed to know something about him, of course, but Imogen had burned her boats as far as using her as a source of information was concerned. She would simply have to be patient.

Discounting this particular personal aspect of the situation, she knew the possibility of a job couldn't have come at a better time. She rather suspected she would have decided to stay in Steynhurst for the foreseeable future to look after Aunt Sophie and family anyway, even before Daniel's unexpected offer. But now she had the chance to maintain her links with serious nursing at the same time, and earn a little extra money into the bargain.

All things considered, it was a very lucky break.

Assuming she could do the job and the practice would have her, of course. She could officially resign from her hospital job and accept the twilight nursing post on offer.

The waiting-room was almost empty when she arrived at the health centre just before seven.

'You're very late,' said the receptionist. 'Have you

an appointment?' She was rather brisk and looked tired at the end of a long day.

'Well, I have,' said Imogen tentatively, 'but it's not to see any doctor as a patient. My name is Moore, Imogen Moore. I'm here for an interview.'

The receptionist's face cleared, and she flashed Imogen a smile. 'Of course, it's about the new twilight nursing post. Dr Granger left word that you were coming.' She looked at the list in front of her. 'He's still with a patient at the moment, but it's his last one and he'll be free after that. Just take a seat, will you?'

A few minutes later Daniel appeared from an inner room with his patient. He looked large and protective, his dark, handsome head inclined solicitously as he bent over to speak to the little old lady who was with him. Imogen's treacherous heart lurched at the sight of him, but she managed to control the blush that threatened to rise to her cheeks and outwardly appear calm.

As he escorted his elderly patient, who was limping slightly, to the outer door of the waiting-room Imogen, who was sitting near the door, heard him say in his deep voice. 'Now, Mrs Bird, in future, if you can't get here in the morning, you must ask me to visit you. I don't like you walking here at night.'

The old lady smiled up at him as they stood in the doorway. 'It's only a step, Doctor, and I'm not a bit nervous, but I was worried about that silly old ulcer on my leg. It seemed to get worse during the day— that's why I left it so late.'

'Well, the new dressing that I've put on and those other tablets that you're going to collect from the chemist should help. Take care, now.' He opened the door and watched as his elderly patient made her way to the pharmacy on the opposite side of the square.

He closed the door and walked over to Imogen. 'I am pleased to see you,' he said, his voice warm with sincerity. 'I half wondered whether you'd come, as you seemed rather uncertain this morning.'

'I was, and I still am, but I said I'd come.'

'And you're a lady who keeps her word,' he said lightly, teasingly, his hazel eyes brilliant.

'Always,' said Imogen firmly, returning his smile.

'Good.' He steered her from the waiting-room into the wide corridor lined with doctors' offices and other rooms. 'The patient who has just left,' he said as they made their way down the corridor, 'is just the sort of person I had in mind for an evening visit. She has an ulcerated leg, which is healing slowly but which tends to flare up at times. If there was a nurse on call it would save her a trip to the surgery after dark, and keep the numbers in the waiting-room down, allowing me and my colleagues time for more urgent cases. Don't you think that that makes sense?'

'It certainly sounds like it, especially if the nurse on duty would be in a position to make treatment decisions on the spot if she was with a patient.'

'Within certain limits she would, and of course she would be able to get advice by phone if necessary, to discuss possible treatment.' They had reached the end of the corridor and he opened a door to a large room furnished with easy-chairs and occasional tables. 'Our staff-room,' he explained. 'Where we all meet up for coffee or whatever and exchange notes on patients. Do come in and sit down; the others will be here shortly.'

'How very comfortable,' said Imogen, taking a chair. 'You do yourselves proud.'

'We decided that if we looked after the staff and ourselves, the health centre would tick over better, and this has proved to be true. We're a very happy group here, we support each other, and it makes for much more efficiency all round. Everyone, down to the cleaning ladies, is involved in making the centre work.' He sat down in an easy-chair opposite her and leaned forward. 'But what we have been lacking, Imogen,' he said, seeming to linger over each syllable, 'is this evening care. The day nursing staff cover most evenings here in the centre, but, understandably, can't stretch themselves to visiting.'

'Presumably you intend employing more than one twilight nurse? I couldn't do every evening.'

'Of course. We have an advert in the local weekly due out tomorrow, from which we hope to get a good few replies. We expect to take on two, maybe three nurses to provide proper cover and relieve each other. But stumbling across you, as it were, is a bonus.' His eyes met hers steadily. 'I know, from what you have done for your godmother, that you are a jolly good nurse. You have provided me with a practical reference, so to speak. What more can I or my colleagues ask?'

The door opened before Imogen, blushing faintly at his praise, could reply, and two middle-aged men entered and were introduced by Daniel as Nick Raymond and Gerry Forbes. They were doctors from other practices working from the health centre. In quick succession, within the next ten minutes, half a dozen people, including Judith Watts, the centre manager, appeared and were introduced to Imogen. Expecting to be overwhelmed by the number of people who had turned up to scrutinise her, Imogen found herself unexpectedly warming to them all.

The informal chat or interview itself seemed casual in the extreme, with everyone drinking coffee and questions being tossed at her in a friendly fashion. It was only as the session progressed that she realised that the apparent informality concealed much shrewd probing of personality and attitude. Purely academically, she was well qualified for the post, but that was not all it required.

The rest of the practice team were obviously favourably impressed by Daniel's prior assessment of her ability and credentials, which he had passed on to them, but they still wanted to be sure for themselves that she was right for the job *as a person*.

Eventually all the questioners were satisfied, and Imogen was quietly pleased to see a number of approving glances and nods being exchanged between the various members of the team; she felt in her bones that the position was hers if she wanted it. And in her heart she realised that the job was right for her, and she for the job.

'So,' Daniel asked, for the record, apparently speaking for all those present, 'if we offer you the job, do you want to join us, Imogen?'

There was no point in pretending to hesitate. 'Yes, please,' she replied simply. 'But I have to officially resign from Bromfield, so I don't think that I could start till next week.'

'Then I think I can speak for my colleagues and say that the job is yours on a trial basis,' said Daniel briskly. 'Come in tomorrow and iron out any problems like contracts and uniforms and written references with Judith.'

'Yes, give me a ring in the morning and we'll fix a time,' said the manager with a nice smile. 'And welcome aboard. It'll be great having you.'

There was a general murmur of agreement, and one or two people started to say their goodnights and leave, while others grouped themselves together to chat and finish their drinks.

Daniel came over and perched himself on the arm of Imogen's chair and looked down at her with a quirky smile hovering round his lips. 'Are you glad you braved Daniel in the lion's den and decided to give us a try?' he asked, gently teasing her. For a moment she wondered if he had guessed at the reservations she'd had about working with him.

'Very.'

'No reservations about coping with the work involved?'

'None,' she said firmly, sure at that moment, with the adrenaline flowing at the prospect of her new job, that she could cope with anything, even on the personal level. Her work would keep her busy and she would be equally responsible to all the other doctors besides Daniel. There was no reason why she couldn't keep him at arm's length should the need arise, though hopefully that wouldn't be necessary. Tonight he had behaved impeccably, being friendly and welcoming, but nothing more, and there was no reason why that shouldn't remain the case. Their future working relationship should be perfectly innocent and harmonious.

She smiled up at him, conscious of his closeness, yet at that moment confident of not being overwhelmed by him. 'I must thank you for putting me up for the job,' she said quietly. 'I'm most grateful. I promise not to let you down.'

'I'm sure you won't. I have every confidence in you.'

'Thank you. Now I'd better go home and give Aunt Sophie the good news—she'll be bursting with curiosity.'

'Did you come by car?' he asked. 'I don't remember

seeing it when I showed Mrs Bird out.'

'No, I walked. It's such a lovely night; the moon's coming up and the stars are out, and it isn't very far from Aunt Sophie's to here, as you know. I thought that the exercise and fresh air would steady my nerves before the interview.'

'I didn't think you had nerves,' said Daniel with a throaty chuckle. 'And I'm afraid your moon and stars have disappeared.' He gestured towards the window. 'Listen, it's absolutely belting down with rain. A March wind with a torrential April shower thrown in for good measure.'

Sure enough, rain was beating violently against the window-panes.

Imogen pulled a face. 'I'll have to get a taxi,' she said. 'May I use the phone?'

'Certainly not—I shall run you home. I'm on call, but relatively free as from this moment.'

'I don't want to put you to any bother.'

'It's no bother; a pleasure.' His hazel eyes smiled down at her.

She wondered briefly if it would be sensible to refuse his offer, and not get into close proximity to him, but with her new-found confidence decided that she could enjoy his company without being overpowered by his presence. 'Thank you, I'll just go and say my goodbyes.' She stood up and moved across to where the centre manager and two doctors were talking, and apologised for interrupting. 'I'm going home now,' she explained. 'Thank you for making me so welcome. I'll ring you in the morning, Judith.'

'Yes, please do that, Imogen. Goodnight.'

One of the doctors asked, 'How are you getting home? Do you want a lift?'

'No, thanks, Dr Granger is taking me.'

Daniel, having put on a raincoat and with his surgical case in hand, was at her elbow as she left the staff-room. 'Nice crowd, aren't they?' he said.

'They certainly are. I'm so looking forward to joining them.'

'The sentiment's mutual.'

They reached the outside door of the waiting-room. 'Wait here,' he commanded. 'I'll bring the car round. There's no point in both of us getting wet.' He turned up the collar of his raincoat and stepped out into the teeth of the storm and was lost to view in the darkness as he made for the staff parking area tucked round the corner.

Imogen stood at the door, shivering. She wished that she were wearing trousers and sensible shoes, instead of the dark suit and court shoes that had seemed right for her interview, however informal. Within minutes, Daniel drove up to where she was waiting. 'Jump in,' he said sharply, pushing wide the passenger door of the Range Rover.

'Thanks.' Imogen climbed into the seat, aware of the length of leg that she was showing, but dismissing it. Surely Daniel wouldn't notice in the wind and the rain?

Unknowingly turning her thoughts upside-down, he said with a broad smile, 'You're not very sensibly dressed for this weather in that elegant suit, are you? Though it's very proper, just right for an interview. I was impressed.'

She felt herself blushing at the compliment, but recovered herself quickly. 'Well, it seems that your colleagues were too, since they're prepared to give me a trial run.'

'You bowled them over with more than wearing the

right clothes. You did it with your natural confidence and professional expertise.'

Imogen laughed. 'Oh, is that what I did?' she said. 'I thought I was just being myself.'

'You couldn't be anything better,' said Daniel, giving her a smiling sideways glance before starting the engine. 'Now, let's get you home.'

Aunt Sophie's olde-worlde book-cum-craft-shop, aptly called BOOKCRAFT, lay at the top of the steeply rising High Street, which was a long, narrow road dividing the town in two from top to bottom of the hill. The new health centre was situated in a cobbled square just off the High Street at the foot of the hill. Although it was a fifteen-minute walk, it took only a few minutes in the car, and Imogen, staring out of the streaming windows, was grateful to be warm and dry.

There hadn't been time for much conversation on the short drive, but as they drew up at the private entrance to the house Daniel asked, 'Does it remind you of anything, all this rain?'

Imogen shook her head, puzzling over what he meant. 'No,' she said. 'Should it?'

'The supermarket,' he replied softly, 'when we first met, and you looked very vulnerable with your fringe dripping raindrops into your lovely blue eyes. I remember thinking what a shame it was that a pretty young mum with a large family had to struggle all by herself with a mountain of shopping. It was the sort of chore that a loving husband might help with.'

For a moment Imogen froze. This was totally unexpected, that Daniel would take advantage of the pleasant evening they had spent by being over-friendly, over-familiar, and reminding her in the most eloquent way of that first meeting and the help that he'd given her. The last thing she wanted now, having said yes to the job, was to be reminded of the impact that he had made at that first and then their subsequent meetings. Though of course, to give him the benefit of the doubt, he probably wasn't aware of this.

Best to play it cool. From somewhere deep inside her she dragged up a casual laugh. 'But I wasn't a busy young mum.'

'No,' he said, surprisingly vehement. 'By God, you were not. You were—are, as far as I know—a fancy-free young woman, are you not, Imogen?' There was a half-question in his voice.

'Yes,' said Imogen, '*I'm* fancy-free.' She emphasised the 'I'm'. Surely he would get the message that would tell him that she didn't consider him a free man? Surely she didn't have to spell it out for him?

He switched on the courtesy light in the car and turned and looked straight at her. 'I'm very pleased to hear it,' he said in a firm, matter-of-fact voice which surprised her. For some reason she had expected a more seductive, suggestive tone. 'Too many people commit themselves when they are too young. It seems such a pity.' The thought flashed through her head that he might be referring to himself and his own marital situation. Perhaps he had married too young and was about to use that as an excuse to deceive his wife, wherever she was. She had another surprise when he put a tentative hand to her cheek and stroked it gently. 'Plenty of time for commitment,' he said quietly, seriously. 'Don't rush things, Imogen, even if pressed, and especially not to please other people.'

She gaped at him. What on earth was he talking about? He was speaking as if what he was saying had nothing to do with himself, but somebody else. What on earth did he mean by that enigmatic warning? And what did it have to do with him anyway—even if she was attracted to him, he wasn't free to reciprocate? He was nothing more than an acquaintance, and a recent one at that.

Confusion made her angry, and her anger boiled up. Why on earth had he spoilt a perfectly good evening, and just as she was beginning to feel that some sort of secure future lay ahead of her and that he and she might be friends? A future in which she could be useful to her beloved godmother and pursue a nursing career of her own.

She breathed in deeply, and said very formally, 'I don't know what you're talking about, Dr Granger, but whatever you're trying to say has nothing to do with you. Now I'll say goodnight, and thank you for the lift.' She made to undo her seatbelt, but Daniel put a restraining hand over hers and undid it for her. She shivered, partly at his touch, partly with temper.

'Now I've made you angry,' he said ruefully, his usually brilliant hazel eyes sombre. 'Which was the last thing I meant to do. Don't let us part on a sour note. Just accept that what I said was for the best, and I didn't mean to distress you.'

He seemed genuinely regretful. 'Just what did you mean?' Imogen asked, her anger beginning to ebb.

His wide, well-shaped mouth parted in a tender smile, and even white teeth gleamed in the dimmish light of the car. 'I meant that you must protect yourself from your own generosity,' he said softly. 'Don't let people take too great an advantage of that generous heart of yours.'

'I don't know what you mean,' she said, further confused and surprised.

'I mean it's quite obvious, from what I've seen and what Mrs Jackson has said, how much you've put yourself out to help the family.' He looked at her narrowly. 'Even to the extent of putting your own career at risk. . .'

A sudden wild possibility struck Imogen. 'This twilight nursing job *is* genuine? I mean, it's not some sort of charity position you've created just to. . .'

Daniel was chuckling, not unkindly. 'Do you really think the whole practice would allow themselves to be part of such a waste of time and resources? No, it's absolutely genuine; only the timing is fortuitous. I am simply very glad that you are so suitable for the job.' He grinned again, with an almost boyish look on his face. 'Perhaps I simply believe that good deeds deserve their just reward. Heaven knows, there's little enough of that in the world.'

His manner was so open and frank that Imogen found it hard to doubt him. At least, she thought with a sigh of relief, he doesn't want to be involved with me. I must have misjudged his words and actions, as he obviously didn't mean anything by them. Maybe he's just one of these tactile people, naturally given to closeness, which explains the warmth of his handshake, and the eye contact that we had. The thought both relieved and vaguely disappointed her. Her mind in a whirl, but feeling bold on account of his apparent willingness to talk in depth, she was braving herself to ask about his own family life, when his phone buzzed.

Daniel grimaced and picked it up. 'Yes?' he said. Imogen could hear a female voice at the other end of the phone, but couldn't distinguish what was being said. 'OK,' he replied. 'I'll go straight over, but Bramling is some way off, so it'll take me a little while to get there. Ring them back and tell them that I'm on my way. See you when I can, and be a darling and keep my supper warm.'

He rang off and pulled a face at Imogen. 'I'm truly sorry, my dear Imogen; end of evening, I'm afraid. That was my mother relaying a call to see a sick baby—sounds serious.' He looked hard, straight-faced, almost a different man. 'It illustrates perfectly why we need a twilight nurse to relieve us doctors of some of our more straightforward cases. I can't tell you how much I am looking forward to having you on the team.' He managed a tight smile, but his air of easy-going charm had vanished with his concern for the infant he was to visit. Yet again he was illustrating what an excellent doctor he was, she thought, always putting his patients first.

Imogen gathered her scattered wits. She didn't know what to make of the last few minutes. Daniel had been tender and very protective when he'd spoken to her. But was he almost too protective for a man with family commitments? She wished they had not been interrupted just then. In another minute she might have taken advantage of his openness by playing the reciprocal card and found out something more about his personal situation.

She wanted him to be genuine and blameless, and she hoped desperately there was no ulterior motive for his apparent concern. But the moment had been lost, and now he was all that could be asked of a responsible doctor—mature, thoughtful, serious. Her questions would have to wait for another time.

'And I look forward to joining the health centre too,' she said in reply. 'Thank you for bringing me home; it was kind of you.' She made to open the door.

Again Daniel placed his hand over hers. 'Don't forget what I said,' he murmured. 'Don't let that generous heart of yours rule your life completely.'

Imogen said quietly, 'No, I won't.' She got out of

the car. 'Good luck with your baby,' she said as she closed the door.

'Thanks.' He put the car into reverse and backed out into the High Street.

Imogen stood for a moment in the pouring rain, watching as his tail-lights receded, then she turned and let herself into the house.

CHAPTER FOUR

FOR Imogen, the period following her interview at the health centre was a curious one, and she felt herself to be in a kind of limbo for much of the time, cutting herself off from one lifestyle and starting another. She sent her letter of resignation to Bromfield and arranged for her friend Lucy Peters, with whom she shared a flat, to send on the rest of her belongings and seek out a new flatmate. 'I'll pay my share of the rent until you find someone else,' she told Lucy over the phone one evening. To which Lucy replied that there wouldn't be any problem about re-letting her room as there was a queue of people waiting to take up any accommodation going. 'But I'll miss you, Imogen,' she said. 'I hope you're doing the right thing, giving up hospital nursing and losing the chance of making sister.'

'So do I,' replied Imogen. 'Hope I'm doing the right thing, I mean. But I am effectively getting promotion to sister; all the trained nursing staff at the centre are elevated to sister's rank, and if I want to stay with Aunt Sophie for a while I must give this job a try.'

'Good luck, then,' said Lucy. 'Keep in touch.'

'I will—bye.'

As she put the phone down a wave of nostalgia for Bromfield, and all her friends there, washed over her. I must be mad, she thought, to do this, change course at this stage in my career. Suppose it doesn't work out, this twilight nursing job; then I'll have nothing left. She shivered, and resolutely put the thought from her. There's no turning back now, she reminded herself, you're committed, and you want to do this job. It was true; the more she thought about it and recalled Daniel Granger's passionate enthusiasm for having a nurse in this capacity, the more certain she was that she was doing the right thing. Steynhurst Health Centre was already a superb example of what community medicine should be and she could contribute to that. And, whispered a small voice from somewhere deep in her consciousness, work beside Daniel and see him regularly. Her heartbeat quickened at the thought, but she forced herself to ignore it.

On the home front she felt that she was on an emotional switchback too. Aunt Sophie was delighted that she was to start nursing, as she put it, 'properly again, not just looking after an old crock like me'. But Laurie had been scathing, almost hostile.

'We've just begun to establish a nice little routine here,' he said bitterly, 'and now you're going to upset it. The children like having you here in the evenings, Imogen, helping them with their homework and making them feel secure. I think it's too bad of you to go swanning off to other people's homes, helping them when you should be helping us.'

'It'll only be for a few evenings a week,' explained Imogen patiently, and, remembering Daniel Granger's words, added, 'After all, it's up to you as their father to provide the twins with security, not me.'

'Well, it's not only the twins who'll miss you, I'll miss you too,' said Laurie, looking intently at her. 'I've enjoyed our games of Scrabble and Trivial Pursuit and so on—they've helped to take my mind off things.' And he added rather pathetically, 'I've been happier recently than at any time since I returned from the States, and it's all down to you.'

Imogen felt a twinge of guilt. Was she really letting

him down? Common sense told her that she wasn't. She'd still be around and his mother was always present, and surely Laurie couldn't set such great store by playing a few board games? She said cheerfully, 'Your mother's great at both games, Laurie. She'll always be willing to play.'

'It's not the same,' he replied, 'you must know that; you're special.' He stared at her again in a way that made her feel vaguely uncomfortable but even more aware that it was sensible to pursue her own course. 'And what about when my work becomes full-time? I won't be home till late most evenings and what will the children do then? After all, that's why you came here, to look after us as well as my mother. Aren't you being a bit selfish taking this on?'

Imogen felt drained. She hadn't expected quite so much opposition from Laurie. Was she being self-centred? Was she taking the job at the health centre more to see something of Daniel Granger than for any other reason? Should she concentrate solely on Aunt Sophie and the Jackson family, and would the children suffer if she started work? The questions seemed endless and her answers to them uncertain. She would dearly have liked to talk to someone about her problems, someone like Aunt Sophie or Daniel, for instance, practical, balanced people, but they were no good; they were part of the problem.

Daniel. . .again she recalled his sensible words warning her about just this sort of situation. Was he right? Was it only because Laurie was in a vulnerable state that he was making these demands of her. . .was he getting too dependent upon her, liking her too much? Well, she would compromise; that was the best solution, and that way nobody would get hurt.

'Laurie,' she promised, 'if there's a problem when

you start full-time work I'll review the situation, but until then, with Aunt Sophie's blessing, and Pam willing to do more hours, I shall do some nursing on my own account and take up this interesting post that's been offered to me.' She met his eyes squarely and refused to give in to the pleading expression that she saw in them. 'My mind is made up,' she said, firmly but gently. 'I don't want to discuss it further.'

The morning following this conversation there was a large delivery of books to the shop, and, leaving Doreen to serve customers, Imogen and Laurie went through to the office to sort and check them.

It was the sort of job that Imogen would normally have enjoyed, examining new titles and discussing window displays, but on this particular occasion she had no wish to be closeted in private with Laurie. He had continued to look pathetic that morning at breakfast, and in spite of her firm words she felt her resolution to continue with her career faltering.

He tried, as she had feared, to bring the matter up again once they were in the office, and only a long incoming telephone call prevented him from doing so.

Relieved at the interruption, Imogen began unpacking the boxes, stacking the books in neat rows on the floor ready for checking. She was working in the narrow space between the desk and the wall when Laurie finished his phone call and put out a hand and touched her shoulder. At that very moment there was a tap at the half-open door, and Imogen, just about to shrug off Laurie's hand, looked up from her crouching position and froze. Daniel was standing in the doorway. Her heart seemed to stand still.

His eyes looked amused. 'Good morning,' he said in his deep, mellow voice.

Somehow Imogen found her tongue and murmured a reply, but Laurie, seeming not in the least disconcerted, removed his hand slowly from her shoulder, and said coolly, 'To what do we owe the pleasure of this visit, Doctor?'

Imogen instantly realised the reason for this cheerless greeting: Laurie was blaming Daniel for luring her away from the family.

It seemed an age before Daniel answered, as his eyes swept round the small room, taking everything in, before coming to rest on her. His mouth lifted at one corner in a half-smile. 'I've been visiting your mother, Mr Jackson. I wanted a word with Imogen about medication and so on. I went into the shop and Doreen told me you were both busy in here.' The half-smile deepened and he raised his left eyebrow. Was he being sarcastic suggesting that they were simply enjoying being alone together rather than busy? The spot where Laurie's hand had rested on her shoulder seemed to burn as Daniel continued, 'And of course I can see that you are extremely busy, so I won't take up much of your time.'

Imogen found herself unconsciously drinking in every detail about him, from his charcoal-grey suit, blue-striped shirt and navy blue tie with a small red motif to his highly polished black shoes and darkly gleaming hair. She had never seen him look so formal, so distinguished, more like a consultant than a country doctor. By comparison she felt almost carelessly dressed in her mid-length cotton skirt and flowery blouse.

Slowly Imogen stood up and brushed her hair back with a hand that, infuriatingly, shook slightly. She was annoyed with herself. She mustn't let him affect her in this manner. Boldly she looked straight at him, and his hazel eyes, when they met hers, changed from being amused to being dark, and quite unfathomable. He looked suddenly serious. Why was he looking like that? He'd said that he wanted to speak to her about Aunt Sophie; could it be that he had bad news about her condition. . .was she perhaps not as well as she seemed? Was there something wrong that she herself had overlooked? For the last few days she had been immersed in her own affairs. Had this made her less than alert to her godmother's condition?

'Is Aunt Sophie all right?' she asked, trying to keep the anxiety out of her voice.

'Yes, she's fine. All down to your good nursing, she tells me, and the gentle exercise and massage that you're giving her. She's certainly more mobile than she was, and generally she's improving, but it was about her injections that I wanted a word. Her latest blood tests show a much better haemoglobin count, so we can decrease her injections but keep up the folic acid. I've made a note here and written up a new prescription.' He handed her two pieces of paper.

There was another knock at the door and Doreen appeared. 'Could you come, Laurie?' she said. 'There's a customer who wants to make an order for some rather obscure books and I think you'd better deal with it.'

Laurie made an impatient noise in his throat and stood up. He looked hard at Daniel as he squeezed past him. 'Excuse me,' he said, his voice heavily sarcastic. 'I have to go, but I'm sure that you can discuss Mother's condition quite satisfactorily with Imogen. She is, after all, her responsibility at the moment, though she seems hell-bent on abandoning her for your health centre.'

'Oh, I don't think so,' said Daniel pleasantly.

'Imogen has much too fine a conscience to allow her own concerns to overshadow your mother's, or, for that matter, yours. But I'm only too happy to talk to Imogen—it's all medical stuff anyway.'

He had moved further into the room to allow Laurie to pass him and was now standing very close to Imogen. She was conscious of his closeness, of his maleness, of the scent of his astringent cologne. He made Laurie seem pale and insignificant by comparison. She put hands behind her back and clasped them together to stop them trembling. This is ridiculous, she thought, I haven't felt like this about a man since I was a teenager. Why is he having such an effect on me?

Laurie disappeared into the corridor.

The office after he had left was suddenly deathly quiet. Imogen felt breathless. Daniel's arm touched her and she turned her head and looked up at him. For a moment their eyes locked together. His were intensely green. They stared at each other. Daniel leaned towards her. Surely he wasn't going to kiss her? She dragged her eyes away from his, bent down and picked up a book from the pile on the floor.

Daniel frowned and moved a step away.

Imogen felt foolish. She had let her imagination run away with her. Of course, that look had meant nothing to him.

'I wanted a word about your duties tomorrow night when you start at the centre,' he said in his deep, firm voice. 'Sorry to talk shop even before you report for duty, but I wanted to put you in the picture about a patient, a rather special patient whom I want you to visit, only I won't be around when you start work tomorrow and won't be able to advise you then.'

'Oh, I see,' said Imogen, feeling a hollowness settle

inside her at the thought that she wouldn't be seeing him. She sat down at the desk and shuffled aimlessly through a pile of invoices.

'I'm off to a GP conference in London which starts this afternoon and ends tomorrow night, so I won't be back until late tomorrow, or even the following day,' he explained.

She was conscious of his eyes still on her, and longed to look up again and lose herself in their hazel-green depths. She made an effort to pull herself together. 'Who did you particularly want me to see?'

'A small boy at the local children's home; he's diabetic and partially deaf, and only five years old. He's been ill-treated and abandoned and is still in a state of shock. He's not emotionally ready to come to the surgery among a lot of strangers—the poor little chap's had enough upheaval in the last few weeks. He seems to trust, as much as he trusts anybody, Sue Forsythe, the senior housemother at the home. She's very well qualified and great with the children—in fact, she's a wonderful person.'

'Couldn't this Sue Forsythe attend to the child?'

'No, I feel that someone experienced in handling a syringe is called for to give him his injections for the time being, as well as monitoring the glucose levels in his urine and blood. He has quite extensive residual bruising, too, from when he was battered, so injections have to be given with skill and care. And I want to extend the range of people whom he trusts, both from a physical and psychological angle. I think that you and Sue between you may achieve something.'

'Well, of course I will do whatever is necessary. Poor little chap, he desperately needs tender loving care, doesn't he?'

'Without a doubt.'

'I'll do my best.'

'I'm sure you will. I'll leave his notes out in my office together with those of several others on the list. See whoever you can tomorrow and the rest the next evening—that is, of course, if you don't get any emergencies to deal with.'

'What's you little diabetic boy's name?'

'Jonathan—Jonathan Butterworth. Do what you can for him, Imogen. He needs a champion.'

'He certainly does.' She smiled at him. He really was a very good and kind doctor, and she couldn't believe that he would be anything but a good family man. There must be some reasonable, innocent explanation for his, at times, intimate manner towards her.

'Well, I must away now,' he said. 'I've got a lot to do before I depart for London and the conference.'

'I'm sure you have.'

Again their eyes met with what seemed to Imogen a curious intensity. Then slowly Daniel moved towards the door. 'I wish I didn't have to rush away,' he said softly, a note of deep regret in his voice. 'I'd like to have put you more in the picture about the children's home, perhaps taken you there myself on your first visit. It's rather special to me. But Sue will give you all the gen. You can rely on her utterly.'

'I'm sure I can,' Imogen breathed in a whisper, unable, unwilling to break the eye contact with him, thrilling to it and regretting it at one and the same time. We shouldn't be doing this, she thought, but couldn't drag her eyes away from his.

Daniel saluted her from the doorway. 'Bye,' he said abruptly, and disappeared into the corridor.

Imogen sat at the desk, staring at the spot where he had stood. She couldn't really take in what had happened, or even if it had really happened. Their silent, magical exchange had seemed endless, though it had lasted only seconds. His eyes had spoken volumes, but what had they said? How could two people who were only briefly acquainted over a matter of weeks experience this deep, almost primitive exchange of emotion? As before, she wondered if it had really happened the way she recalled it. Had his look been so intense, so full of things unsaid? Perhaps, after all, it *was* only in her imagination. Because she was attracted to him maybe she misread the signs. Maybe the intensity that she thought she saw in his eyes only mirrored her own feelings. It was an unpleasant and unwelcome thought, and the sooner she pulled herself together and became her usual practical self, the better.

Abruptly she pushed back the chair and thumped her closed fists down on the desktop. 'Damn, damn, damn,' she said fiercely. 'Damn the man. I will not let him make a fool of me. I'll just get on with my work here, and at the health centre, and keep away from him as much as possible. He may be a smashing doctor, but I don't think much of his ethics as a man, so there.' She glared down at the invoice in front of her and thumped the table again, then winced as a pain shot through her right wrist. Ruefully she rubbed it with her left hand, and managed a small, bitter smile. 'I jolly well will make a success of things,' she muttered, 'in spite of the Daniels and Lauries of this world. To hell with all men.'

Somehow she got through the rest of the day, so cool with Laurie that eventually he stopped trying to pester her about changing her decision to do domiciliary nursing.

The following morning she went as arranged to the

health centre to meet up with one of the community nurses and accompany her to the various homes that she would be visiting on her own that evening. The only place they didn't call at was the children's home. 'Daniel called there this morning before going off to London,' explained the nurse, 'so little Jonathan doesn't need to be seen till this evening for his second injection. And, of course, it's not the same as going into a private home. Sue Forsythe or one of her deputies will be expecting you, and will introduce you to Jonathan.'

When Imogen reported for work that evening Judith Watts, the manager, went through the list of people that the various doctors wanted her to see. There were six plus Jonathan. Four were patients whom she had seen that morning, needing a general check-up, help to bed and treatment to pressure areas, and two needed wounds redressed and pain-relieving injections given.

As her preparations for her visits had taken some time on this first evening, and it was after half-past five when she left the centre, Imogen decided to see Jonathan first and the other patients later.

Gable End, the children's home, lay on the outskirts of the town, a one-time country mansion surrounded by many acres of parkland. A dozen estate cottages had been enlarged to accommodate houseparents and several children in a homely atmosphere, while the main building remained a reception area with facilities for accommodating difficult or sick children and babies. Here, newly admitted, often traumatised youngsters were cared for by Sue Forsythe and specially trained helpers, before moving into foster homes or the cottages in the grounds.

It was a fine spring evening and still bright with a brilliant sun beginning to set in the west when Imogen arrived. She pulled up on the wide sweep of drive in front of the main entrance door that stood open in a sort of welcoming fashion. Several children were playing on the lawn beside the drive, accompanied by two adults, a man and a woman.

The woman detached herself from the group as Imogen got out of the car and came over to speak to her.

'Hi,' she greeted Imogen cheerfully. 'You must be the new nursing sister that we've heard about. I'm Jane Cooper, Sue's assistant.'

They shook hands and Imogen introduced herself.

'Sue's inside with Jonathan,' said Jane. 'He's a bit tearful because he knows that Dr Daniel isn't coming to give his injection, but he often is, poor kid, weepy or withdrawn. Not surprising, of course, given his history, but give us time and Sue's particular brand of magic and we might work a miracle.'

'Sue Forsythe sounds a rather special kind of person,' said Imogen, following Jane into the wide hall of the house. 'Dr Granger was full of praise for her.'

Jane laughed. 'Well, he would be, wouldn't he?' she said, giving Imogen a meaningful glance. 'But it's true anyway—Sue is special. . .most of us who work here would do anything for her. She's made Gable End a byword in child care.'

She led Imogen across the reception hall with its black and white tiled floor and slightly shabby but comfortable-looking furnishings. A large, squashy settee and a couple of matching chintz-covered armchairs were arranged in front of the old-fashioned stone fireplace. It would look warmly welcoming in the winter with a log fire blazing away; now it looked bright and cheerful with a huge bowl of daffodils and narcissi filling the empty grate. To complete the homely picture, children's drawings festooned the walls and a few toys lay scattered about the floor and on low tables. A real home, thought Imogen, unfrightening and reassuring to a child arriving in need of care and affection. No wonder it had such a good reputation with the authorities and the medical and social services.

There was a wide, shallow staircase leading up from the hall, with a safety wicket gate at the bottom and the top. 'To prevent our tinies coming to grief,' Jane said as she led the way up the stairs to the first floor and into a large airy room on the right of the landing.

'This is a sort of office-cum-consulting-room,' she explained, 'where Dr Daniel sees the children when he comes on his weekly visit. As you probably know, he is the home's medical officer.'

This was news to Imogen. 'No, I didn't know that,' she said, 'though I knew, of course, that he looked after Jonathan. I just thought each doctor had their own patients here.'

'Most of them come here from time to time doing locum for him, but he's definitely the boss, and the children love him, even some of the tough ones. He seems to have a special rapport with them.'

Imogen smiled. 'I'll bet he does,' she said, rather more warmly than she had intended, then hastily looked at her watch. 'Will Jonathan be long? He should have his injection soon.'

Jane said, 'Sue'll be here with him any minute. She knows you are due, and won't be late, but I'll just. . .' She broke off as the door opened, and a smile broke out over her face. 'And here she is,' she said with relief.

Imogen hadn't been sure what she expected Sue Forsythe to be like, but she certainly hadn't envisaged the slim beauty who confronted her. Sue had a cloud of fine auburn hair floating round her face in a tangle of small curls, and brilliant green eyes. She was leading a small boy by the hand.

She advanced towards Imogen. 'You're Imogen, of course—Sister Moore; Daniel's told me all about you. I'm sure that you're going to be a wonderful asset to the centre. A twilight nurse. . .it sounds lovely, doesn't it, all calm and reassuring, like tidying up the nursery before the children go to sleep?' She gave Imogen a dimpling smile and gently pushed the small boy forward. 'This is Jonathan,' she continued. 'Who isn't really looking forward to meeting you, because he knows that you have to give him his injection. But because he's brave and sensible he knows that the injection is necessary to keep him well.' She crouched down and spoke to the small boy, who was standing mutely between her and Imogen. 'That's right, Jonathan, isn't it?'

Jonathan nodded and mumbled, 'Yes, but I don't like my needle pricks.'

'I don't think anybody likes needle pricks, Jonathan,' said Imogen softly, also crouching so that she was on his level. 'But sometimes the pricks are less of a bother than not having them, because they stop you from getting ill.'

Jonathan stared at her through tearful eyes. 'I don't like to hurt,' he said.

'Of course you don't, so I promise I'll be very gentle.'

'Have you done these pricks before?'

'Oh, yes, hundreds of times.'

'Hundreds and hundreds?'

'Yes.' She squashed a temptation to say dozens rather than hundreds, feeling that her slight exaggeration was justified.

'Well, I'll let you do it, then,' said Jonathan.

Imogen tested the boy's blood with the machine that took a spot of blood to establish the glucose level, and then drew up the necessary insulin in a syringe with a fine needle. 'I'm going to clean your arm with this antiseptic swab,' she explained, suiting action to words, deliberately being very matter-of-fact. 'And then pop the needle in like this.' Carefully, smoothly, she slid the needle into the child's thin arm and discharged the insulin through it. She withdrew the needle, swabbed the arm again and smiled at Jonathan. 'All done,' she said. 'Now, what are you going to have for supper, poppet?'

'A Marmite sandwich and half a glass of milk,' said Jonathan promptly. 'If I'm allowed.' He looked rather wistful.

'That sounds great. And perhaps half an apple,' said Imogen. 'Just right for tonight.'

'Thank goodness for that,' said Sue with a sigh of relief. 'Our Jonathan has a passion for Marmite sandwiches, haven't you, love?' she said to him, giving him a gentle squeeze round his thin shoulders. 'And I hate to refuse him.'

'He needs that amount of carbohydrate tonight,' replied Imogen, smiling at Jonathan and receiving a rather tremulous smile in reply, 'and the milk. Children are particularly difficult to monitor as they use up energy in such bursts, but Daniel seems to have got this chap's levels just right.'

'I'm sure he has,' said Sue. 'He's very perceptive where children's needs are concerned.'

'So I believe. From everything that I've heard he's great with all the children.'

'His extended family, he calls them. Treats them as if they were his own. He's very generous; buys them

toys and things, much beyond the call of duty, but
there's no stopping him.'

The words hit Imogen like a sledgehammer. For a
moment she thought that her heart was going to stop
beating. She drew a deep steadying breath. 'Does he
sometimes go out on a nappy-buying spree?' she asked
faintly, trying to sound normal and humorous at the
same time.

Sue laughed. 'As a general rule he wouldn't shop
for something quite so basic, but he did a few weeks
ago when we were near to running out and our new
supplies hadn't arrived. He'll do anything for the kids.'

Imogen's heartbeats were now so hard and fast that
she was sure that Sue could hear them, and she felt
the blood coming and going in her cheeks as a great
wave of relief swamped over her. After all her doubts
here was the simple, innocent truth. Daniel Granger's
only 'family' commitment was to the Gable End
children's home!

She was for the moment at a loss for words, still
reeling from the sense of relief with which Sue's explanation had filled her. It was Jonathan who broke
the spell.

''Scuse me,' he said, tugging at her arm. Imogen
looked down at him. His large brown eyes for some
reason reminded her of Daniel's hazel ones, but
Jonathan's looked soft and serious, too serious for
those of a five-year-old child. 'Can I have my supper
now?' he asked. 'I'm ever so hungry.'

Imogen looked at Sue, who smiled and nodded.
'Right away,' said Imogen. 'Where do you go for
supper?'

'To the big kitchen. Rosie gives it to us.'

'Then I suggest that you whizz off and get it, if Sue
thinks it all right.'

'Fine,' said Sue. She patted Jonathan's shoulder. 'Run along, love, and tell Rosie to give you your usual.'

Jonathan made for the door, but turned as he reached it and said solemnly to Imogen, 'Thank you for doing my injection. It didn't hardly hurt at all, just like when Dr Daniel does it. You can do it again if you like.'

'Thank you, I'll take you up on that.'

Jonathan nodded and disappeared through the doorway, leaving Imogen and Sue exchanging uncertain smiles.

'A satisfied customer,' said Sue. 'And praise indeed to be linked with Daniel.'

'I understand that he's rather special here.'

'His word is virtually law, unless it happens to clash with mine.'

'I can't believe that that happens often.'

'No, hardly ever; we're on the same wavelength where Gable End is concerned,' said Sue.

'I can believe that,' said Imogen, thinking that Daniel would be almost certain to go along with Sue in most things in connection with the children. She looked at her watch, trying to be purposeful and businesslike in spite of the elation still glowing within herself after the recent revelation. 'Well, I must be off now, as I've other patients to see.'

'I thought that I might show you around, since it's your first visit.'

'I would like that, but some other time perhaps—I really must go now.'

'Right, I'll see you out. I'm glad you were a success with Jonathan, but then, Daniel forecast that you would be.'

'Did he indeed? Well, I'm glad he was right—I wouldn't want to disappoint him.'

Sue pulled a comic face. 'Nobody does,' she said; 'that's his strength, that everyone wants to please him.'

They walked down the gracious, shallow staircase and crossed the hall to the front door.

Imogen paused at the door and held out her hand. 'Goodbye,' she said. 'I'm so glad we've met. I'll see you and Jonathan tomorrow.'

'Goodbye.' Sue returned Imogen's handshake with a nice firm grip. 'We'll look forward to that.'

The evening was beginning to close in and a purple dusk was settling over the parkland as Imogen crossed the drive to her car. The children who had been playing on the grass when she had arrived had disappeared, presumably having gone in to supper. Sue stood outlined in the doorway against a halo of light from the hall, epitomising all that was good about the children's home. Imogen thought rather fancifully, This really is twilight nursing; dusk is falling, night's just about to descend, and everything's quiet.

The quiet at that moment was shattered by an engine changing gear as it climbed the drive, and a pair of headlights pierced the half-light. Some quivering expectant sixth sense told Imogen that it was Daniel Granger who was arriving, and a moment later his Range Rover pulled out from the tree-lined drive and stopped beside her own car.

Before he could switch off the engine Sue had hurried across from the hall door. 'It's Daniel,' she said happily to Imogen, who was just about to get into her own car, but hesitated. Should she stay and see him? She very much wanted to. It seemed an age since yesterday morning when they'd parted at the shop, and then she hadn't known, as she did now, that he was a free man. Her pulse bounded as her mind grappled with this novel idea.

She said hesitantly, 'I'd better get on, and I expect you and Daniel will want to talk.'

Sue laughed. 'There are always things to talk about where the children are concerned, but do hang on and have a word with him yourself. He'll want to know about Jonathan.'

Daniel opened the door of the Range Rover and stepped out.

'Evening, ladies,' he said, smiling at both women. He had removed his jacket and loosened his sober-looking tie for the drive home. He stretched his shirtsleeved arms above his head in a natural gesture of relief, and taut-looking muscles across his broad shoulders and upper arms rippled beneath the silk of his shirt. 'London is unbelievably dreary and dirty after this lovely countryside,' he said, breathing in a lungful of fresh night air. 'I escaped from the last monumentally boring lecture and so got back earlier than expected.'

'And naturally made a beeline for Gable End,' said Sue, looking pleased.

'Naturally.'

Imogen noted that they smiled at each other in the way that people who were close did, as if there was more to the words used than had actually been spoken. She wished that Sue hadn't persuaded her to wait and speak to Daniel, as she felt superfluous to the two of them.

'Look, I must be off. . . I've the rest of my list to do, and I can't afford to be late on my first evening,' she said, fitting the key into the lock of her car, and giving Daniel a shy smile. 'My bosses wouldn't like it.'

'This boss would forgive you,' said Daniel, his eyes twinkling. He put a hand over hers, and stopped her turning the key. 'But just tell me how you got on with Jonathan, please.'

'Oh, fine. He was chary of me at first, but with Sue's help I gave him his blood test and his glucose level was OK, so I gave him the insulin that you'd prescribed. He's now having his favourite supper. . .'

'I know—a Marmite sandwich and half a cup of milk,' said Daniel with a grin. 'Such a simple meal, but he counts it almost as a treat. Pleasure, like everything else, I suppose, is relative. Jonathan had so few treats when he was in what passed for home.' He lifted his hand from Imogen's and she turned the key in the lock, unfastened the door and quickly seated herself.

'I'll leave you my report on Jonathan and your other patients on your desk,' she said as she switched on the ignition and put the car into gear.

'Thank you; see you tomorrow. Goodnight, Imogen.' He stepped back to stand beside Sue, and draped a casual arm round her shoulders.

As she moved slowly off over the sweep of gravel in front of the house Imogen could see them both reflected in her mirror. Two stunningly attractive people standing intimately side by side, secure in their companionship.

She turned down the drive and they were out of sight. Imogen felt tears pricking the backs of her eyes, and she muttered angrily at herself. For almost five wonderful minutes she had been able to believe that Daniel was free and had compromised no one by his gentle advances towards her. Advances? Was that the right word? Well, what did it matter now?

Because she realised that Daniel might not have a family in the ordinary sense, but clearly, with Sue Forsythe and the children, he had a ready-made one right here at Gable End. They were obviously attracted to each other, and looked so right together. There was no doubt about it. She'd seen it with her own eyes.

And yet, perhaps there was still a chance.

Daniel obviously thought of himself as a free agent or he wouldn't have allowed himself to behave as he had towards her. He had let her know that he felt something for her emotionally. It had all seemed so intense and. . .well, *honest*. Her heartbeat quickened as her mind took on board the exciting thought.

After letting one misunderstanding almost rule her life for many days, she was not going to make the same mistake again.

Everything seems in the balance, she thought, and I mustn't do anything to spoil it. If Daniel and Sue are a serious item, then I won't help them or me by forcing myself between them—and anyway, I wouldn't want him if he makes advances, however smoothly, behind her back. But if they are, like that worn old cliché, 'just good friends', then I'll simply have to wait and see.

Imogen reached the bottom of the drive and turned on to the road into town. With great determination she suppressed all her personal thoughts. She had a job to do, other patients to visit, and she must concentrate on them to the exclusion of all else. Time enough to dream when she got home.

And dare to hope, she added.

CHAPTER FIVE

'IMOGEN.' Daniel's deep voice rang out clearly across
the car park as Imogen prepared to leave for her
evening visits. 'Hang on a minute.'

Imogen opened her car door, squashed the little
wave of excitement that his voice had precipitated, and
waited for him to join her. She wondered what it was
that he had to say to her. It was four days since their
meeting at Gable End, and, though she had seen him
briefly to discuss patients from time to time since then,
they hadn't exchanged a personal word. In fact she
had begun to wonder if he was avoiding her. True, he
was usually busy in his consulting-room or was out on
calls when she came on duty, but, whereas the other
doctors had made a point of asking how she was settling
into her new job, Daniel hadn't said a word. It was
as if, having succeeded in persuading her to join the
centre, he had now washed his hands of her. Not, she
told herself, that she wanted any special treatment
from him, but it would have been nice if he had shown
continued interest. Ironically, she had even missed seeing him at home when he had visited Aunt Sophie the
previous day as she had been out shopping. Was any
of this significant, or merely coincidence?

She glanced at her watch as Daniel approached. She
had already been delayed by one of the other doctors.
It was a little before six o'clock and a bright April
evening with a washed blue sky dotted with fluffy
clouds arching above the centre, contrasting vividly
with the red roof-tiles. A smattering of early blossoms

decorated the cherry and almond trees that surrounded the car park, and a splash of scarlet tulips in the flower borders beneath the windows heralded the late spring.

Daniel crossed the tarmac in long easy strides. His dark hair gleamed in the evening sunlight. He stopped and looked down at her, tall and vital in fawn cord trousers and a tweedy jacket with leather patches at the elbows, worn over a dark shirt and tie. A countryman's outfit, thought Imogen, and how well it suits his broad shoulders and narrow hips. He looks so absolutely right in it, casual, very contemporary, like someone out of *Country Life*, yet approachable too and utterly dependable. No wonder he's so popular with his patients.

In spite of her disappointment at his apparent neglect of her and her determination to be cool and collected, she found herself smiling a welcome. She looked up at him as he stood in front of her, automatically taking in every detail of his face. It was a face that was too craggy to be conventionally handsome, with its high cheekbones and strong jawline, but it was an attractive, masculine face, with sensitive lines about the mouth and eyes.

'Hi,' she said quietly, very aware of being close to him, longing to put up a hand and softly touch that firm jaw, that sensitive mouth. With a mental jerk she quelled the extraordinary desire. 'I've got the notes you left about Mr Churchill,' she said briskly. 'Was there something else you wanted to tell me, Doctor?'

Daniel's brilliant hazel eyes twinkled. 'Doctor! My goodness, we are being formal. No, nothing specific. I just wondered how you were getting on. We seem to have been passing like ships in the night lately, but then, we've both been busy.'

'Yes, we have, and I'm getting on fine, thank you.' So he hadn't forgotten or avoided her. Tentatively she brushed at her fringe with her fingers and was conscious that the gesture was a nervous one caused by his nearness, by the sound of his voice and the expression in his eyes. The knowledge made her cross with herself and, for some obscure reason, with him. She lifted her chin and met his twinkling gaze with cool eyes. 'Well, if that's all,' she continued, 'I'll be on my way. I've a long list of people to see tonight.'

'You've only two others of mine to see besides Jonathan; Prue Wright, my hypersensitive middle-aged lady, a ripe candidate for a stroke, and Mr Churchill.'

The arrogance of the man. 'But also two patients of Ray's and three of Nick's,' she pointed out. You're not the only doctor here, you know.' She tried to keep her voice light and brittle and rather distant, but as always when Daniel mentioned his patients his face and voice had softened and she was reminded of what a caring person he was, and she felt herself responding. He wasn't really arrogant, just focused on his own patients.

Daniel pulled a face, and then gave her a wry smile. 'Hey, don't be so spiky, Imogen. I didn't suppose that I was the only medic with calls on your time, but surely a few minutes' conversation isn't impossible? I'm only concerned about your progress since you joined us and wanted to know if you're happy in your work. For my part, I'm delighted with how well things are working out. We're getting great patient feedback from those folks who find it difficult to get to the surgery. This evening nursing help is going like a bomb. It's certainly filling a gap.'

Imogen felt churlish, knowing that she wanted to rush off less because of the time factor than because she found him disturbing. She capitulated and returned his smile, 'Yes, of course I can spare a few minutes,' she said. 'And it's kind of you to be interested.'

'Rubbish,' he growled. 'I got you into this, so the least I can do is to keep an eye on my protégée.' To her surprise, he suddenly put out a hand and flipped the fringe of her chestnut-brown hair. 'Getting long,' he said softly. 'Needs cutting.'

'I know,' said Imogen. There was a tremor in her voice. She made an effort not to be affected by his touch, or at least not to let him see that she was affected. It was ridiculous and infuriating. She forced herself to be calm and casual and ran a careless hand through her hair. 'I've got an appointment with my hairdresser tomorrow. Not,' she added, deliberately tart, 'that it's any of your business.'

Daniel laughed. 'Are you sure?' he said softly. 'Perhaps as one of your employers I have a right to insist on a neat, well-cut coiffeur for our beautiful nursing sister—for purely professional reasons, of course.' He paused and added in a low tone, 'or even unprofessional ones! I, personally, like your fringe short and bouncy. . .it brings out the violet-blue of your eyes. Such kind eyes, with such a gentle expression in them.' His own eyes were bright and teasing, but his voice was infinitely tender.

The fact that he had noticed the length of her fringe and the colour of her eyes brought a flush of rose-red to her normally peaches-and-cream cheeks. This conversation, she thought, has gone far enough. It's full of innuendo, full of things best left unsaid, unless they're sincerely meant. Was he just doing a little harmless flirting, or did he mean them? Her mind whirled. She felt almost out of her depth. She wanted to return things to a normal, even keel, dismiss something over which she had no control.

'Look,' she said sharply, glancing again at her watch,

'I really must get on...my patients will be getting impatient.'

The small pun was meant to bring the conversation to an amicable end, but Daniel seemed to be surprised or offended by it. The expression on his face changed subtly; the laughter went out of his eyes, and he became brisk and efficient.

'Of course,' he agreed, his voice expressionless. 'I shouldn't have detained you. You've plenty to do, and so have I, for that matter, so this is no time for silly chit-chat. What a good job we've got two more nurses starting next week—you'll be able to get some well-deserved time off. I'm sure you need it.'

'I'll be glad of that, as Aunt Sophie and Laurie and the children still need me at home occasionally. I shouldn't do more than four evenings a week, however much I enjoy it.'

Daniel's expression changed again. He frowned. 'Of course they need you,' he said, sounding impatient. 'But don't be afraid to do your own thing, Imogen, however much they mean to you. You owe it to yourself.'

Imogen slid into the driving seat of her car and Daniel rested his lean, brown, competent hands on the half-open door.

She looked up at him. He had changed yet again. He was neither brisk nor impatient now, his expression soft and compassionate, like the face he wore when he spoke of his patients. But the expression in his eyes was special, tender, intimate, and, she felt, for her alone. She swallowed. 'I won't,' she said, 'forget to do my own thing.'

He nodded. 'Good.' He straightened up, and then, dismissing all things personal, smoothly slipped again into his professional role. 'Now when you see Prue

Wright will you take her BP at the beginning and the end of your visit, allowing as much time in between as possible? See if you can get something like an accurate reading; her blood-pressure, always high, is up and down like a yo-yo. She ought to be hospitalised; trying to rest at home isn't really good enough, but she won't leave her father. Do try and persuade her. Tell her we'll get Social Services to do more for him, and I'm sure some of the neighbours would help out if they knew the problems. At worst we can get Mr Wright into a home for a week or two so that she can go into hospital and at least be stabilised.'

'I'll do my best,' she promised, somehow managing to sound professional too, though her mind was busy turning over his earlier remarks and the look on his face which had seemed to convey so much. She fastened her seatbelt, switched on the engine, and closed the door.

Daniel bent down and looked through the open window. 'I'm sure that you will, Imogen. I can't imagine you ever doing less than your best.' He stood up and patted the top of the car. 'Off you go, now. Drive carefully.' He raised a hand, turned and walked back across the tarmac, and after a moment disappeared through the swing doors of Reception without a backward glance.

Her mind an absolute maelstrom of muddled thoughts, which she strove to squash, Imogen drove away out of the car park to start her visits.

By the time she reached Gable End to see Jonathan, the first patient on her list, she had got full control of herself and was ready to concentrate on her work. She found him happily playing with another small boy, and quite ready to have his blood test done and receive his insulin injection with his new friend looking on with interest. Jonathan was in fact a different boy to the frightened waif she had first visited a few days before.

Sue was delighted with his progress. 'Now that he's made a friend for himself,' she told Imogen, 'if he follows the usual pattern he'll begin to open up to other people. The first step always has to come from the child himself, and when it does happen it's often quite sudden. Before long he'll settle in school and begin to integrate properly.'

'I bet Daniel's pleased with Jonathan's improvement both physically and psychologically,' Imogen said, deliberately bringing Daniel's name into the conversation, wanting to see what reaction there was, if any, from Sue. She felt oddly self-conscious and experienced a little glow of pleasure as she said his name, and recalled what had passed between them at the health centre.

Sue, of course, was quite ignorant of her thoughts. She said cheerfully, 'No, he doesn't know it's happened yet. It was only this afternoon that Jonathan suddenly decided to make friends with Tim, but he will be thrilled about it. He has this wonderful rapport with most of the children, but particularly with Jonathan.' Her smile changed and grew tender, softer, as she spoke of Daniel.

'Yes, he has, hasn't he?' said Imogen.

A few minutes later she said her goodbyes to Sue and drove away from Gable End, deep in thought.

She was sure that Sue was very deeply fond of, if not actually in love with Daniel; the look on her face when she spoke of him revealed that. But how intensely did he reciprocate those feelings? He admired her, and they seemed so *close* when they were together, but was that enough? And why, if he is actually in love with Sue, does he seem to be interested in me? her jumbled thoughts queried.

Is he simply playing the field, or just being over-friendly? Or is he a natural flirt? I wonder if he has any of the sensations that I have when we are near each other? But if he does, is that significant. . .is it anything more than just a sort of chemical reaction on both our parts, a purely sexual attraction? He must know what a charismatic effect he has on women, so is he being cruel or being kind to me, knowing how he's affecting me?

She squirmed at the thought. Yet the other morning in the office, this evening in the car park, the extraordinary expression on his face, in his eyes. . .surely she hadn't imagined all of that? Surely it meant something more than biological attraction?

Ruthlessly she pushed these thoughts out of her mind, ashamed at having allowed herself to dwell on personal matters when she should be concentrating on work.

She took the road back towards Steynhurst, and, consulting her list, decided to visit Mr Churchill next, who, as he lived on the outskirts of the town, was the nearest patient.

Mr Churchill was a recent below-knee amputee, having lost the lower part of his leg in an accident in which it had been badly crushed. He was an elderly man who lived with his equally elderly wife, and he was waiting for a new prosthesis to be fitted to his stump, which was sore and slow to heal properly.

Imogen concentrated her thoughts on this problem as she pulled up in front of Mr Churchill's bungalow in a quiet tree-lined road. Tonight she would start the new treatment which she had discussed with Daniel.

In fact it was old-fashioned treatment, rubbing the stump with soap and spirit to improve the circulation, before applying a simple, soothing cream. To date they had used several new and expensive applications to promote improvement, but without success. And until the stump improved and a limb was fitted the old man was virtually chair-bound, as he found it difficult to cope with crutches.

Mrs Churchill let Imogen in. 'He's by the fire as usual,' she said in a strained voice, 'and very bad-tempered and fed up today. I do hope, Sister, you can do something for him. I can't stand much more of this.' She looked near to tears.

'Well, Dr Granger wants your husband to start on some new treatment tonight, and I'm sure it's going to help. I'll be doing it each evening and the day sister will do it in the morning.'

Mrs Churchill cheered up a little. 'Oh, I do hope so. He's just had about as much as he can take, what with the accident and everything, and so have I. I could kill those joyriders who caused all this.' Her little lined faced looked savage for a moment.

She led the way into the small, neat sitting-room where Mr Churchill sat looking lopsided, uncomfortable and morose. He barely answered Imogen's greeting, or noticed how she automatically rearranged his cushions and straightened him up. He just nodded when she explained about the new treatment. No wonder, thought Imogen, his wife is near to breaking-point if he's been like this all day. It was a plain illustration of how the carer suffered when there was long-term disability in the home.

The carers needed a lot of support and sympathy, which was partly what this twilight nursing was about— to help the whole household cope with a chronic situation; to be a visitor who would in turn care and understand.

She attended first to the small open suture wound that hadn't quite healed. 'That's doing fine,' she said, swabbing it gently before re-packing the tiny cavity with ribbon gauze and covering it with a light dressing to ensure that it healed from within. 'Now let's get going on the stump.'

Twenty minutes later she left the Churchills both in a happier state of mind. Mr Churchill actually agreed that his stump felt more comfortable after treatment, which cheered Mrs Churchill immensely. 'I think he'll be happy to watch the telly now that you've made him comfortable, Sister,' she said as she escorted Imogen to the door. 'And I certainly feel better for your visit; you're such a cheerful, reassuring young woman.'

Warmed by this reaction to her visit, Imogen made her way to her next patient, a nearly blind, nervous lady recently returned from hospital following a hip replacement.

Dr Raymond had asked her to check that Mrs Taylor was comfortable and clear about her night medication and pain-killers. 'She gets a bit confused at times,' he'd explained, 'so I've only written her up for a little sedation, but I'd hate her to mix up her sleeping tablets with the Co-Dydramol for the pain. As you know, they're quite different in size, and in colour, but she can't easily distinguish this. Perhaps it would be a good idea to leave out two of her night tablets and four pain-killers, and put the rest away somewhere safe till the morning.'

She wasn't long with Mrs Taylor, whose niece, Brenda, had unexpectedly turned up with plans to stay for a few days. It was quite a relief to find that the old lady wasn't on her own. Imogen was able to leave instructions with Brenda, an obviously sensible young woman, about her aunt's medication, and move on to her next appointment.

It was almost dark when she drove away from Mrs Taylor's terraced house facing the green, and, though the sky was clear, it was quite gloomy beneath the trees coming newly into leaf. Imogen switched on her headlights, for it was that time between day and night when visibility was poor. A few children still played on the swings and slides, and a group of boys kicked a football aimlessly about in the growing darkness.

Imogen drove cautiously along the road that encircled the green with a wary eye on the boys, who were moving towards the edge of the grass. At any moment, she thought, they're going to kick that ball on to the road. She was coming up to the short inter-section that divided the green into north and south sections.

There wasn't a lot of traffic about at this time of the evening in this largely residential area, but there was some movement round the pretty thatched pub that dominated one corner of the green.

As she approached, slowed down and signalled that she was turning right, a car started to turn from the pub car park just ahead of her, and another car turned out at some speed from the intersection and came towards her. It was at that moment that the football hit Imogen's car bonnet with a loud smack, and bounced off on to the road in front of the car leaving the pub. Both Imogen and that driver swerved, and, as both were going slowly, quickly brought their vehicles under control and to a stop. But the car coming towards Imogen failed to slow down, the driver seem-ing to be unaware of what had happened. It was as it drew nearly level with her that Imogen, to her horror, saw that one of the boys was about to dash into the road after the ball.

'No, don't!' she shouted uselessly as the boy darted out from between the trees that ringed the green into the path of the oncoming vehicle.

There was a screech of brakes as the car tried to stop and slewed to one side, and a loud, dull thump as the boy collided with it. Imogen, frozen in her seat, viewing the scene as if in slow motion, saw the boy flung into the air on impact and fall with a heavy thud on to the ground.

It seemed an age before she could move, but it was seconds only. She took a few deep breaths as she undid her seatbelt with controlled fingers, and automatically checked that the road was clear before stepping out of the car and running across to where the boy lay.

She knelt down beside him. He looked about twelve or thirteen. He was lying flat on his back with his eyes closed and a trickle of blood and clear fluid oozing from his nose and one ear. He looked pathetically fragile and pale. Imogen felt his wrist for a radial pulse, and found one, weak and thready and fast. The man who had been slowly driving from the pub car park appeared beside her.

'Is he. . .is he dead?' he asked shakily.

Imogen shook her head. 'No, but he may be injured internally. Now, please phone for an ambulance and the police, then come back and look at the driver of the car that hit him, as he may be hurt too.'

The man nodded and moved away at once towards the pub, from which a number of people had emerged. He seemed quite prepared to take orders from her— obviously her nursing uniform lent her authority. Dimly she heard him say something and then he was back beside her.

'Someone's phoning,' he said. He looked pale, but was obviously in control. 'I'll go and look at that chap now, Nurse.'

'Right, if he's bent over the steering-wheel, don't move him, just tell me.'

'OK.' He moved over to the car.

The boys who had been playing football stood bunched at the side of the road looking frightened.

'How is he, Nurse?' one of them called.

'He's unconscious. What's his name?'

'Mark.'

'Mark.' Imogen bent over the still form. 'Can you hear me, Mark?' There was no response. Imogen turned to the boys. 'Will one of you fetch the rug from my car? You'll find it on the back seat—and bring the case that's on the front seat.' Again she took Mark's pulse. It was still fast and thready. Automatically she noted that his respirations were shallow but reasonably steady. She lifted his eyelids to examine the pupils, but in the dim light couldn't see if they were equal or not.

A boy arrived with the blanket and her case. 'Can I do anything else?' he asked. 'Shall I go and tell his mum what's happened?'

Imogen covered the injured boy with the blanket. 'Does he live far from here?'

''Bout five minutes away.'

Was it best to wait for the police to carry the news, or would their arrival later be more distressing to Mark's mother? 'All right,' she said, then added firmly, 'But be sure to tell her *first* that Mark is all right and being taken care of and the ambulance has been sent for. Don't frighten her by making it sound worse than it is, understand?' The boy nodded and started to run off, another of the boys following him. 'And go carefully!' Imogen shouted after him. 'One accident is enough for today!' The boys slowed down to a brisk jog. 'The rest of you, wait for the police, to give them what information you can, but meanwhile one of you fetch my torch from the glove compartment.'

'OK, Nurse,' another said eagerly, clearly pleased to have something to do.

The man who had offered assistance, and was looking at the car driver, reappeared. 'He's conscious,' he said. 'He spoke to me, but he seems to have hurt his neck when he tried to stop. It sounds like a whiplash injury. Is there anything I can do for him?'

'Keep him as quiet and straight as possible. If you can find anything suitable, make supports for either side of his head to keep it still, and keep him warm with a rug or extra coat. He's bound to be shocked.'

'Right.' He went back to the car.

Imogen knew that there was very little she could do for the injured boy; he almost certainly had a skull injury—the trickle of fluid from his ear indicated that. The boy started coughing fitfully. If he was having difficulty breathing then she would have to turn him. Even though she had examined him as best she could, there was always a chance he had some spinal injury that movement would aggravate. Still, he had to breathe, and if his coughing became more violent that alone might cause damage. She prayed that the ambulance would come soon.

At that moment somebody crouched down beside her, and she saw as she turned that it was Daniel. A great wave of relief washed over her as she took in his calm and reassuring presence.

'Oh, I'm so glad you're here,' she murmured thankfully. She swallowed. The relief at having someone to share the responsibility with was enormous. She looked down at Mark. 'I've given him a quick examination

and can't find any obvious injury except to his head.
I was just going to cover his ear with a pad and get
him into the recovery position to keep his airways free.
I can't think of anything else to do, can you?'

Daniel shook his head. 'Not a thing, my dear; you've
got everything under control.' Even as he spoke he
was running gentle hands over the boy's neck and
torso, looking for possible damage. 'No, nothing else
that I can find, but you're right, we'll have to risk
aggravating his possible skull injury and put him in the
recovery position to ensure that he can breathe.'

Between them, they very gently secured a dry sterile
pad over the boy's left ear with a light bandage, then
with infinite care, supporting his head, rolled him on
to his left side. Carefully they tilted his chin upwards
to keep his airways free, and then bent his right leg
across his left leg until his knee and foot touched the
ground to help support the angled weight of his body.
He was in the classic recovery position, enabling him
to breathe freely once more. They covered him with
the blanket.

Daniel examined his eyes with a pencil torch that
he took from his top pocket. 'Pupils uneven,' he said.
'You're right, a possible skull fracture, but perhaps
not a severe one.' He took both the radial and temporal
pulses again, and confirmed that they were still rapid
and thready. 'There's nothing anyone can do now until
the ambulance arrives,' he said quietly. 'You stay here
with the boy and I'll go and look at the car driver.'

'I haven't seen him,' Imogen said, 'but it sounds as
if he might have a whiplash injury. I told the chap
who has been helping me to keep him still and support
his neck.'

'Right, I'll check.' He squeezed her shoulder.
'You've done wonderfully well,' he said softly. 'Keep

it up till the ambulance comes—it won't be long now.'
He seemed to understand that she was feeling the strain
of dealing with the badly injured boy. Superficially she
was professional, but deep down she felt as anyone
might, seeing a young life threatened.

Imogen nodded and watched his tall figure stride
across to the car that had hit the boy. She could have
wept with gratitude at having him close by to support
and sustain her, he was so calm and unruffled, yet at
the same time so warm and caring.

She remained kneeling beside Mark, talking to him
softly and monitoring his pulse-rate and respirations,
and praying that the ambulance would soon arrive.
Her prayers were answered minutes later, when both
the ambulance and a police car appeared and she was
able to hand over to the emergency crew.

As soon as they arrived Daniel came over to speak
to her as she was returning her case and rug to her
car. 'I've got to go now,' he said. 'I'm out on a call—
not urgent, a check-up on someone I saw this morning,
but I don't want to keep her waiting any longer than
I have to. Will you be all right, dealing with the police
and so on?'

'Of course; you get off, and thank you for coming
to my rescue.'

'You didn't need rescuing, you were managing perfectly well in your usual calm and efficient way.'

Imogen shook her head. 'I didn't feel very calm and
efficient. It's years since I worked on Casualty, and
then it was only as a student. I was terrified of doing
something wrong, or overlooking something.'

'Well, you didn't, take my word for it.' He was
standing very close to her beside the car. She could
feel the heat from his body and smell the peculiarly
medical mixture of cologne and antiseptic soap that

emanated from him. In the near-darkness they seemed isolated from the buzz of activity going on a few yards away, where the emergency team was loading the patients into the ambulance and the police were talking to the boys. His arm brushed hers, and, in spite of all that had happened and the horror of the accident, she felt a thrill of pleasure at his touch, and drew in a shuddering breath.

He caught her hand lightly in his and squeezed her fingers gently. 'Imogen,' his voice was husky and deeper than usual, 'I have to go now, but we must meet some time.'

'We meet nearly every day,' she said softly with a tiny laugh, trying to ease her own tension, knowing what he meant, deliberately teasing, feeling suddenly light and happy at his words and the tone of his voice.

'Only at work,' he growled, 'and that's not what I call meeting. I'll phone you tomorrow and we'll make a date for dinner one evening. Now I'm off—goodbye.' He turned away abruptly, without waiting for her to reply, walked a few steps and then turned back to face her again. 'By the way,' he said quietly, 'take Prue Wright off your list. She lives near my next patient and I'll see her myself. You're going to be hard pressed to finish tonight. Take care, love; you'll be out late.' Even in the dim light shed by car headlamps and the orange glow from the lights that had just come on round the park, she could see his faint smile, the gentle set of his mobile mouth.

She could sense his concern.

He really cared. Her heart thumped painfully, joyfully. 'I will,' she whispered.

He nodded, raised a hand and walked out of the circle of activity that still surrounded the scene of the accident.

Imogen stared at the spot where Daniel had stood. She felt curiously lightheaded and detached, as if what had happened had happened to somebody else. The ambulance moved off, and a policeman came over to speak to her. She pulled herself together and gave a description of the accident. The policeman asked her to call at the station the next day to make a proper statement, and then she was free to go.

Nearly an hour had passed since she had left Mrs Taylor's house, but it felt longer, so much had been packed into that hour.

She was, she realised, slightly in shock from the strain of taking charge at the accident and slightly featherheaded on account of Daniel. Adrenaline and professionalism had kept her going when it mattered, but now that the crisis was over she was feeling distinctly rattled and rather tired. More than anything she would like to have gone home and had a strong cup of tea, and slumped in an easy-chair. She reminded herself that this wasn't possible—she still had her work to do, she couldn't let her patients down, and, anyway, Daniel was expecting it of her, he had made that quite clear. A little thing like an accident mustn't interfere with one's work schedule. He drove himself hard and expected his colleagues to do the same. Well, that was all right with her; she had never let a patient down yet, and wasn't about to start now. She squared her shoulders, cleared her mind of all but details connected with her work, consulted her list, and drove to her next appointment.

It was close to eleven o'clock when she arrived home. Aunt Sophie had gone to bed, but Laurie was still in the kitchen.

'You're late,' he said aggressively, directly she

walked in. 'I've been worried about you. You should be home just after ten. Where on earth have you been all this time—chatting up your precious doctor?'

'No. Working,' Imogen replied quietly, realising that genuine concern was making him aggressive. 'I was delayed by an accident.'

'An accident! What sort of an accident? You're not hurt, are you?' he asked, his manner changing immediately, his voice taut with anxiety.

'No, I'm fine. I was only indirectly involved, but I just had to stay and help, that's all. It made me rather late with my visits.'

'Did you have to go visiting after being in an accident? Surely someone else could have taken over? I don't like you out so late; it's not safe. . .even Steynhurst has its yobbos.'

'I have a job to do, Laurie; it's called twilight nursing—that's dusk into dark. And I've told you before, it isn't any of your business what I do. Please don't fuss.' Tiredness made her speak plainly, but his reaction was both warming and flattering.

For a fleeting moment she almost wished that Daniel had suggested her abandoning the rest of her list on account of his concern for her. But it was a brief wish. He put patients first, and knew that she would do the same. He treated her as an equal, and she was glad of it.

With great sincerity, Laurie said, 'I can't help caring about you, Imogen, you've done so much for me and the children since you arrived.'

'Well, I'm glad that I've been useful, but all I want at the moment is my bed.' She gave him a nice smile to take any sting out of her words. 'But thanks for waiting up for me, Laurie. It's nice to come home to a warm welcome.'

Laurie looked pleased. 'You must be worn out,' he said. 'Can I get you anything. . .tea, a milk drink, brandy, anything?'

'A small brandy would be nice. Help me to sleep.'

'Here, take it up with you,' he said, pouring the amber liquid into a small balloon glass. He leaned across the table and planted a light kiss on her cheek. 'Sleep well,' he murmured softly. 'You deserve to.'

Imogen took the glass from him. He really was very kind. 'Thank you,' she said. 'I will. Goodnight.'

She went upstairs to her pretty bedroom. She had expected to lie awake for hours, going over the events of the evening, but the moment that her head touched the pillow, all emotion exhausted, she fell into a deep and dreamless sleep.

CHAPTER SIX

When Imogen awoke the next morning she was conscious of a great wave of happiness sweeping over her. Daniel was going to phone! Her tummy churned with excitement. She couldn't believe how much she was looking forward to hearing from him. What would he say. . .would he just invite her in a straightforward fashion to have a meal with him, or would he refer to their brief but intimate conversation last evening at the scene of the accident?

She made an effort to be matter-of-fact, reminding herself that she was a mature woman who had led a full social life in hospital, and was quite used to going out on dinner dates with men. But those weren't dates with Daniel, said a small voice inside her head; they had been fun, but they hadn't mattered. Whereas this first date with him mattered very much. It shouldn't, but it did. They had been skirting around each other for weeks. She was beginning to know him as a doctor and an employer; now she wanted to know him as a man, she wanted to know what made him tick, where man and doctor merged.

It was strange that, though she didn't know some of the most prosaic things about him, like his taste in music, or whether he took sugar in his tea, in some ways she felt that she had known him forever. Those silent looks that they had exchanged had seemed to *say* so much, right from the beginning and that first day in the shop, when he had caught and held her eyes with his. Had he felt drawn to her as she had to him, by some invisible thread pulling them together? It had seemed a mutual exchange, but was it?

Did it matter? She had his phone call to look forward to.

Her heart pumped erratically at the thought, and she felt herself glowing with happiness as she went to help Aunt Sophie prepare for the day ahead.

Her elation must have been obvious, for Aunt Sophie greeted her with, 'You look in great form this morning, Imogen, especially as you were so late home from work last night. I thought you'd be tired out today.'

'No, I'm not tired, and I wasn't all that late—I was in by eleven. I just got held up, that's all. I'm sorry I wasn't here to help you to bed.'

'That's all right, my dear, Laurie gave me what help I needed. And thanks to your care I don't need much these days. But what made you late?'

'I got involved in an accident——'

'An accident?' Aunt Sophie interrupted in some alarm.

'Oh, I wasn't personally involved, but I had to stay and give first aid and that mucked up my visiting list.'

'Well, thank goodness you weren't hurt, Imogen. We were both rather worried about you when you didn't get back by your usual time. It's silly, I know, but Laurie was especially anxious. He's very attracted to you, my dear, do you realise that? He seems quite suddenly to be resigned to losing Kim, and is looking towards you.' She hesitated and laid a hand on Imogen's arm, and said apologetically, 'I'm sorry, I don't mean to pry into how you feel about him; it's none of my business. But don't hurt him, Imogen, by misleading him. Be honest with him; he's suffered enough.'

'You must know that I wouldn't hurt him intentionally, Aunt Sophie. I've done nothing to encourage him to think that I'm any more than an old friend.'

'Except by being your loving self, Imogen. You're so warm and tender-hearted that he may be reading more into that than you intend, and you're so splendid with the children.'

'Well, I can hardly start pretending not to care for him and the children, can I?' Imogen said rather sharply, and then added gently, 'At the moment he may think he fancies me, but that's only because I'm available, and he's grateful for my help with the twins. Frankly, I think that he's still in love with his wife.'

'Do you?' said Aunt Sophie, an expression of hope flickering across her face. 'Perhaps you're right. Maybe,' she added wistfully, 'there will be a reconciliation, and Kim will come back to him soon.'

'It's possible—let's hope so. Now, what dress are you going to put on today?'

Imogen finished helping Aunt Sophie to dress and managed to keep the conversation away from herself, but she knew that the astute old lady would soon begin to guess at her growing interest in Daniel Granger. Not, she reminded herself, that there was any reason to keep it a secret. She was a free agent, and so was he...

Except for his connection with Sue Forsythe, of course.

She sighed inwardly. That uncertainty still had to be resolved, though how he coped with that was surely his own affair. He had made it clear he wanted to see her, and he wasn't the sort of man to string two women along at the same time...was he? Then it must mean he and Sue really were 'just good friends'. Well, she wouldn't let it worry her. Though she liked Sue and hoped that she wouldn't be hurt, she was looking forward to going out with him. It might be her best chance to learn the truth about where Daniel Granger's affections really lay.

Her earlier euphoria evaporated a little, and a few doubts began to invade her thoughts. Perhaps she was reading too much into his promise to phone, his desire to date her. Perhaps the traumatic events surrounding the accident, and the peculiar ambience that had enveloped them as they parted, had given her a false indication of his feelings. In the cold light of day, it seemed very probable.

As she worked in the shop, and later retired to the kitchen to prepare lunch, she tried to view the situation dispassionately. Perhaps she had imagined the look in his eyes, the huskiness in his voice last night. Perhaps he wouldn't ring at all—after all, it was a casual enough thing to say 'I'll ring you tomorrow'. A lot of people said it, and never did ring.

At that moment the phone rang.

Imogen picked up the receiver. 'Steynhurst five-one-three-four-six-two,' she said steadily.

'Imogen,' said Daniel's deep voice in her ear.

Her heart bounded at the sound of his voice. He had rung, he had kept his promise. She expelled a deep breath.

'Oh, I'm glad that you've phoned,' she said. 'You've just caught me. . .I was about to go shopping.' The small lie tripped off her tongue readily. For some reason she didn't want him to suspect that she had been waiting for his call since early morning.

'But I said that I would ring,' he replied in a rather surprised voice. 'Did you think that I might not?' Before she could answer, he added sharply, 'If I make a promise, I keep it.'

She said lamely, feeling mean, 'Of course, I'm sure you do. It's just that I didn't know when you would ring.'

'I've had a busy surgery, and I assumed that earlier you would have been occupied with helping your aunt and getting the children off to school.'

'Well, yes, I was.'

'So it would have been pointless ringing you at the crack of dawn, would it not?' he said briskly.

'Yes.'

His voice softened. 'Though that's what I would like to have done.'

'Would you really?'

'Yes.'

'Why?'

'Because I spent half the night thinking and worrying about you.'

He had worried about her—how wonderful. Her pulse quickened. 'Why did you worry?'

'Because you were going to be so late finishing your list, and one of your visits was to the flats in Penhurst Place, and even Steynhurst has its rougher elements and most of them live there. It's bad enough in the daytime, but late at night. . .'

'It's nice of you to worry, but it's my job, and whether it's ten or eleven doesn't make much difference surely?'

'Oh, but it does, because the pubs start closing around then and the streets are much more dangerous for women. I should have thought of this before. Perhaps we should consider male nurses for this twilight stint. They could take care of themselves. . .there wouldn't be any problem with them.' He sounded suddenly distant and rather thoughtful and impersonal. 'And,' he added, 'we don't want anything to spoil what is essentially a good idea because you, or the other nurses who will be joining us, have trouble.'

The chauvinistic nerve of the man! Imogen could hardly believe what she was hearing. She felt her anger rising. He was obviously being protective not only of her, but also of his precious scheme. No way was she going to take that and have her job put in jeopardy. 'Look here,' she said fiercely, 'I can take care of myself. My hospital ran self-reliance classes, and I'm pretty good at defending my honour or anything else that's threatened, believe me. No drunken lout or male chauvinist is going to chase me out of my job, and you can bet your boots that these other nurses who are starting next week will feel the same.'

Daniel gave a shout of laughter. 'My dear Imogen,' he said mockingly, 'I didn't realise you were such an ardent feminist—you are far too sweet-tempered and vulnerable for the role.'

Imogen gave a little snort of disgust. 'I am not an ardent feminist in the way that you probably mean it. Extraordinary as it might seem, I quite like men, but on some sort of equal terms. The streets should be safe for everybody. And men get attacked as well, you know! We just can't afford to give in to the bullying element anywhere; we have to make a stand.'

'I couldn't agree more,' he replied, suddenly serious, 'but unfortunately we have to take things as we find them. Anyway, I'm afraid that we must pursue this fascinating subject another time. I have to go out on my rounds, so I just want to fix a date and a time to wine and dine you. Shall we say Saturday night?'

'I'm working; I'm not off till the new nurses join the centre on Monday.'

'Yes, you are. I've asked one of the day nurses to cover for you and she's agreed. So there's no earthly reason why you shouldn't come. I'll pick you up at about seven. Now I must go and get started on my rounds. . .goodbye, Imogen.'

He put the receiver down before she could reply. She could hardly believe it—of all the conceited, male egoists, he must head the list. He seemed to think that just because he had fixed it, she would automatically go out with him. Well, she wasn't sure that she would fit in with his plans, she told herself crossly. . .though in her heart she already knew that she would. The awful, compelling thing was that she wanted to enjoy his undivided attention for one evening, and was willing to pay the price for it in dented pride.

But the planned Saturday night date never materialised.

The packed waiting-room at the health centre the next morning gave ample indication of what was to come, and by the next day it was clear that an intestinal bug, with all its complications, was spreading through the community in a minor epidemic. The staff were soon rushed off their feet, doubly inconvenienced by the fact that some of their own members were also incapacitated by the outbreak.

Every other person seemed to be suffering from diarrhoea and vomiting, and needed advice and treatment. The old and the very young were most at risk from dehydration, and had to be pressed into taking extra fluids. Nobody knew how or from where the epidemic had arisen, or whether it was caused through an unidentified virus or widespread food poisoning of some unknown origin. That would be something for the Ministry of Health to investigate.

Luckily Imogen and Daniel escaped its effects, but the twins and Aunt Sophie were badly affected, and even Laurie suffered a mild attack.

Daniel, like all the other doctors at the centre, had found himself caught up in the outbreak that kept him busy night and day. Imogen hardly even saw him at the surgery, as he was out on calls most of the time.

Her own nursing workload was increased on account of the tummy-bug epidemic, and she was glad of the help of the new nurses who had joined the team.

She was also busy at home. Everyone, even Aunt Sophie, seemed to need constantly bolstering up, but it was Patti in particular who needed Imogen. Like her twin brother, she seemed lethargic and indifferent and had virtually lost her appetite over the last few days; she looked pale and large-eyed and dehydrated. Only Imogen was able to get through to her at all, as with her father and her grandmother she was quiet and withdrawn. But even Imogen could not get her to admit what was really bothering her, though she could guess, of course. All Imogen could do was be with her as much as possible, and, when she was well enough, play endless games of Junior Scrabble, for which she had a passion, encourage her to take fluids, and be ready to listen should Patti want to confide in her.

Busy as she was, mothering the children, helping Aunt Sophie, who was having difficulty walking again, and giving moral support to Laurie, she thought constantly of Daniel.

At a time when they needed to talk, work kept them apart. If only they could have some time together, perhaps they could make sense of the situation. But the mini-epidemic went on relentlessly, and the most she saw of Daniel was glimpses of him crossing the car park, or in the crowded waiting-room as he ushered another patient into his office.

She pretended to herself that it was just as well she

wasn't able to talk to him intimately, since she was in such a turmoil about their tentative relationship and his possible interest in Sue Forsythe; but it was cold comfort, and not really true.

Then, one day when she went on duty, she found Reception only half full, instead of crammed to the doors, and Daniel waiting for her in the doorway of his office as she made her way down the corridor to the duty room.

He smiled at her as she approached and held out his hands in greeting, but in spite of the smile he looked exhausted and haggard, which somehow emphasised his rugged good looks. All doubts for the moment forgotten, Imogen smiled up at him as she took his outstretched hands. 'This is an unexpected pleasure, Doctor,' she said with a little laugh, tingling with excitement at his touch. His fingers on hers were electric. 'Are you sure you've time for such dalliance?'

Daniel pulled her into his office and shut the door. 'I'm going to make time,' he growled, 'for this.' He folded her in his arms, moulding her body to his, and kissed her hard on the mouth. But before she could catch her breath and respond, he lifted his head and said softly, his hazel eyes gleaming greenly, 'That was but a foretaste of things to come. I've had nothing but fleeting glimpses of you recently—you've been working like a Trojan, and you must have been equally busy at home, coping with the twins and Mrs Jackson. Sorry I haven't been able to make another visit since the initial one, but I knew they were in your very competent hands and you would call me if necessary. Thank God, this tummy bug seems to be letting up at last.'

'I thought it might be,' she said as she eased herself out of his arms, unable to think straight when he was

too close, 'with the waiting-room being half empty.
I'm so glad; it's been a beastly time for everyone, and
especially you doctors. You all look worn out.'

'You and the other nurses have done your share.'

'Yes, but we've not been at the sharp end the way
you have.'

'Hey,' he said with a laugh, 'all these compliments,
my ego's going through the roof.' Then he was suddenly serious. 'Now tell me, how are things at home?'

'To be honest, only middling to fair,' she replied.
'Aunt Sophie has stiffened up and her ankles are very
oedematous. I'm massaging them twice a day, and
keeping her legs elevated. The twins are recovering,
but unusually slowly, and Laurie is terribly anxious
about everything and everyone.'

'You've certainly got your hands full.'

'It's the twins I worry about most, Patti especially.
And Laurie, who was beginning to cheer up and give
them support, has gone to pieces again, underlining
the fact that they haven't got a mother to turn to. I'm
better than nothing, which is why I must be around as
much as possible, but I'm a poor substitute, I'm afraid.
After all, we all want our mother around when we are
sick, don't we?'

'Indeed,' he said softly, his eyes gentle with compassion, 'it's the most natural thing in the world. So,
what are we going to do about this situation? There's
got to be an answer somewhere. What about trying to
take advantage of their illness, in a manner of speaking? Couldn't Laurie contact his wife, put her in the
picture about the children, appeal to her maternal
instincts to at least come and visit them?'

'He's adamant about not getting in touch with her.
Said he tried endlessly when they were first separated,
and she just didn't want to know. She seems to be

infatuated with this other man. I think Laurie has given up all hope of a reconciliation.'

'Infatuations usually fade, unlike the real thing.' His eyes met Imogen's and spoke volumes, and her heart thudded with a longing to be in his arms again.

She forced her voice to be steady as she replied, 'Perhaps she thinks it is the real thing; in fact she must do to have left her husband and children on account of it.'

'I think——' He was interrupted by the telephone shrilling sharply. He shrugged and gave Imogen a wry grin. 'Thwarted again. I think this is a call that I've been expecting,' he said. 'I'm afraid it's going to take a little while, as it's about a cancer patient and a body scan, so we'll have to continue this conversation some other time.' He bent across the desk and kissed her swiftly, and picked up the receiver, watching her with a faint smile and a tender expression in his eyes as he did so. 'Bye,' he mouthed silently.

Imogen returned his smile, and went quietly from the room. In spite of their conversation's being interrupted, she felt happier than she had done for days. The kiss had been thrilling, unexpected. She wasn't sure that it was love on his part, but the magic that had flared up on the night of the accident was still there between them. And it had been a great relief to talk to him about the family, for he understood how strong was her commitment to them.

The tummy-bug epidemic slowly diminished, but everyone was still kept busy, catching up on routine work that had been put aside to deal with the emergency.

At home, the twins were a little brighter. Patti's appetite improved somewhat, but they were still far from the happy, carefree children that they should have been.

Daniel called one morning after his return from the hospital, where he had been visiting a patient. Imogen let him in the side-door, her heart beating a tattoo of pleasure at the sight of him.

'I didn't think you'd have time to come,' she said diffidently.

Daniel searched her face with a tender expression in his eyes. 'I made time for my favourite household,' he said, and brushed a kiss across her cheek. 'Though this is a flying visit.'

Imogen felt herself blushing and her eyes glowing. 'I'm so glad you did,' she said with a happy laugh. 'Shall we go up to see the invalids?'

'We'd better,' replied Daniel softly. 'Or I might forget why I've come.'

Imogen led the way up to Patti's room. Daniel gave her a cursory examination, knowing that the true problem was not physical, then asked gently, 'Now, Patti, how do you feel in general?'

'What do you mean, in general?' she replied, wide eyes fixed on Daniel.

'Well, apart from the pain and discomfort that rotten bug has given you, do you feel unwell in any way? Are you particularly worried or unhappy about anything? It's a well-known fact that when people get ill it sometimes highlights another problem. Do you understand what I'm saying?'

'Yeah, I guess I do. You mean is there anything on my mind?'

'Exactly, and is there?'

Her eyes filled with tears, and a small fist tried to scrub them away. At last she said in a wobbly voice, 'I want my mom.'

Imogen, who was standing by the bed, reached out and smoothed the girl's hair back from her forehead. It was an automatic, comforting gesture, but Patti turned her head away sharply.

'Of course you do, love,' said Daniel in a kind but rather brisk voice. 'It's the most natural thing in the world to want her especially now you are ill. It's sad that she's not here. But you're not on your own. There are plenty of people who love you. Your dad, brother, granny and Imogen. You're lucky to have so many people who care for you.'

Imogen thought him almost too cool and detached. She wanted to give the tearful little girl a hug. But this matter-of-fact psychology worked. Patti stared at him for a moment, swallowed her tears, and said in a small but remarkably firm voice, 'I guess so,' and then asked, 'When can I go back to school? It's boring being at home.'

'Next week, but don't do any violent exercise for a few days. Do what Imogen tells you—she knows what's best for you.'

'That's what Dad says. Imogen always knows best.'

'And so she does,' confirmed Daniel, smiling at Imogen over the child's head. 'So you do precisely what she says—promise?'

'OK,' said Patti. 'Promise.'

'Good,' said Daniel, smiling down at her. 'That's my girl.' He levered himself off the side of the bed and moved to the door. 'Now I'm off to see Granny.' He opened the door wide. He glanced across at Imogen and inclined his head. 'After you,' he said softly, his eyes warm and tender.

'Thank you,' she said breathlessly, slipping past him. 'Aunt Sophie is in the sitting-room.'

Aunt Sophie was ensconced in her favourite chair

by one of the windows in the long sitting-room.

'And how are you, Mrs Jackson?' enquired Daniel, taking her arthritic hand gently in his.

'All the better for seeing you at last,' replied Aunt Sophie. 'Not that I'm complaining. It was kind of you to come to see us at all when we started this silly bug; you must have been very busy. I was worried about the children, but I knew that Imogen would call you again if she considered it necessary.'

'Of course she would have done,' said Daniel. 'Now, I understand that you've stiffened up since this tummy upset.'

'Yes, I have a little—it's ridiculous. I thought that at my age I'd be immune to all the minor diseases that go around,' she smiled ruefully, 'but it seems I was wrong. But Imogen's getting me sorted out with massage, and exercise and those wonderful oils she uses. I shall soon be fighting fit again.'

'Let's hope so, Mrs Jackson, or her efforts would have been in vain.'

'No, never that. I don't know what we would have done without her.' Aunt Sophie put out a hand and touched Imogen's arm. 'The dear girl has been a wonderful support. We all depend upon her shamefully. But she must start leading a life of her own soon, I realise that, though I dread losing her.'

'Well, you're not losing me, Aunt Sophie, I'm not going anywhere, so don't worry about it.'

Aunt Sophie turned to Daniel. 'I'm right, aren't I, Daniel?' she said. 'She should start getting out and about a bit, don't you agree?'

'Wholeheartedly.'

'Well, my boy, it'll be up to you—she hardly goes out of the house, except when she's working. She watches over us like a mother hen, and I think she's afraid to leave us to our own devices in case something happens. I'm right, aren't I, Imogen?'

Imogen was surprised at how accurately her god-mother had read her feelings. She shrugged and tried to sound casual. 'It's not that, it's just that I want to see the twins more settled and you a little stronger before I start painting the town red. . .'

'And Laurie a little happier,' interrupted Daniel tersely, his hazel eyes for once hard. 'Your Aunt Sophie's right, Imogen, it's time you had a break. Now that the situation at the centre is easing up we must re-fix our date. I shall be having some free evenings next week, so we'll go out for a meal, or to the cinema, or to the theatre. And we have your aunt's blessing.' He winked at Aunt Sophie. 'That's so, isn't it, Mrs Jackson?'

'It certainly is.'

Imogen opened her mouth to protest, but Daniel said smoothly, 'There we are, Imogen, it's all arranged. I'll phone you and fix the details. Now I must be off, as I've a load of calls to make.' He shook Aunt Sophie's hand. 'Thanks, Mrs Jackson,' he said softly, 'for your support. Goodbye.'

'Goodbye, and thank you for calling.'

Imogen was too cross with both of them to speak. How dared they make arrangements for her time off in such a high-handed manner? She was a woman quite capable of making her own arrangements. The fact that both of them had her welfare at heart did nothing to lessen her fury. She turned her back on the room and stared out of the window.

Daniel crossed the room to the door. 'Come and see me off, Imogen,' he said, 'please!'

Reluctantly Imogen turned from the window. With-out appearing appallingly rude, she could hardly refuse to do so. 'Very well,' she said coldly, and followed him out.

Downstairs in the kitchen he put down his case and took her in his arms before she could protest. He looked down into her cross face, his mouth curved into a half-teasing, half-tender smile. 'Don't be angry,' he murmured, 'because your aunt and I are concerned about you. We can both see that you are becoming too involved, too committed. You're becoming obsessive about caring for the family, and that's not good for you or them.'

Imogen stared up at him for a moment. She shouldn't be in his arms. Yet somehow it seemed so right to be there. She hid her face against his chest. 'I know it's silly, but I simply can't help it. They need me,' she said in a muffled whisper.

'I know,' he replied simply, 'and we must do something about that.' He looked at his watch. 'Lord, I must fly, I'm all behind with my visits. We'll work something out. Goodbye, Imogen.' He gave her a long, hard kiss and was gone.

She stood for a moment in the large, old-fashioned family kitchen, savouring the kiss, staring at the door through which he had disappeared. Everything was happening too fast, she thought. They'd hardly had time to get to know each other—*properly*—and yet he was acting as if he had some sort of rights over her. Or was she reading all the signs wrong? Was he just a warm, tactile, overprotective man who looked upon her as a sort of protégée because he had introduced her to the health centre?

And, over and above all, there was Sue Forsythe! Where *did* she come in the scheme of things? Imogen gave a huge sigh and stared unseeingly out of the window. So many questions. She would have to be patient and wait for time to give her the answers.

On this thought, she resolutely put her problems behind her, and began preparing the lunch.

CHAPTER SEVEN

FOUR days later Imogen, who'd had some long-overdue evenings off, resumed her twilight nursing duties.

She hadn't seen anything of Daniel over her off-duty period, but he had phoned briefly the previous morning, apologising for not having been in touch before. He was still catching up on the backlog of work, he explained, and, to make matters worse, two of the medical staff were away; on top of that, following hot on the heels of the tummy bug there was an outbreak of chickenpox in the flats on the edge of the town.

'It's by no means an epidemic, but keep an eye on the twins,' he advised. 'Let me know at once if they produce any suspect signs and I'll call in and see them officially. And if they do succumb I'm sure that I don't need to tell you to keep them away from your aunt Sophie. . .we don't want her picking up any cross-infection such as shingles.'

'We certainly don't,' she agreed. 'I'll keep an eye on all three of them, and anybody in the district who's in a similar vulnerable position. There are several elderly people living with young families who might be candidates for infection.'

'Good thinking.' There was a slight pause, then he said softly, 'Imogen, on the personal front, I'm afraid there's no chance of fixing our dinner date at present. I've no idea when I'm going to be free. I can't tell you how sorry I am. I was looking forward immensely to wining and dining you, but it's just not on. And even now I must rush off, as I've an awesome number of patients to see this morning. It's so bloody frustrating not being able to see you except in the line of duty. But I'll sort something out soon, never fear. *Au revoir*, my love, take care. See you.'

Suddenly brisk, he had barely waited for her to say goodbye before putting the phone down.

He had called her *his* love. Heart fluttering, pulses racing, Imogen stared at the silent receiver in her hand for a moment and then replaced it on the base. She took a few deep breaths and with a vague hand stroked Bess's soft furry head. 'Well, what do you make of that?' she murmured breathlessly to the sleeping cat. 'It wasn't so much what he said as the way he said it. His voice was so. . . Oh, Bess, I think perhaps he loves me. Wouldn't it be wonderful if he did?'

Bess opened one amber eye and regarded her for a moment. Then stretched, exercised her claws, yawned, and went back to sleep.

The possibility that Daniel might be in love with her simmered in the back of her mind for the rest of the day. And that night, in the darkness, she hugged the possibility to herself and bubbled with quiet happiness.

In the cold light of day, common sense told her that he'd not said anything about being in love with her, just that he wanted to see her. So what about his ongoing relationship with Sue Forsythe, she reminded herself—that couldn't be dismissed out of hand, could it? But even common sense and reason couldn't dispel the aurora of euphoria that wrapped around her.

That evening she arrived at the health centre early and found that there was a long list of people for her to see. It was clear that the evening nursing service was being used to capacity, and the hard-pressed doctors were quite rightly syphoning off patients who didn't need their particular expertise on to the nurses. And quite right too, she told herself as she checked the records of all those patients that she had been asked to visit.

Most of them were straightforward, but Daniel had written against one name on his list, 'See me before visiting'.

Imogen rang reception. 'Is Daniel free?' she asked.

'He's got a patient with him, but should be finished soon,' she was told.

'Right, please let him know that I'm available.'

'Will do, Imogen.'

A few minutes later her phone rang. It was Daniel. 'I hear that you're available,' he said with a chuckle. 'Well, you can come and see me any time, Sister Moore, I'm free.'

She tried, not very successfully, to push down the rising tide of pleasure that swamped her at the thought of seeing him, reminding herself that they were both on duty. She managed to say in a commendably cool voice, 'Do you want me to come now?'

'Now would do admirably,' he said with another chuckle.

She went along to his office and tapped at the door. He opened it immediately. 'What took you so long?' he asked with a grin.

'I came as soon as I could.'

'Did you?'

'Yes.'

Their eyes met and held for an instant. She stood in the doorway, and he drew her into the room and closed the door behind her.

'Imogen,' he said softly, taking her hands in his and drawing her into the room. 'You wanted to see me?'

She said, her voice shaking a little and her breathing uneven, 'You wanted to see *me*, Daniel, about a patient.'

'The devil I did,' he said. 'Who?'

'A Mrs Snow—you wrote "See me" beside her name.'

Daniel grinned. 'So I did,' he squeezed her hands, 'but it was more a ruse to get you alone in my room for a moment to do this. . .' he kissed her lightly on the lips and smiled into her eyes. . .'than because there's much to tell you about this poor lady. Nevertheless, now you're here I'd better fill you in about her.' He gave her another swift kiss that for a moment left her speechless and breathless, and then moved round behind his desk. He sat down and waved a hand for her to do the same. 'Mrs Snow,' he said, 'is a wonderful lady of eighty, with great presence and courage. She has osteoporosis, and her spine is disintegrating fast, so she has great difficulty in walking. She depends on her walking-frame to go even a few yards, taking much of her weight on her arms and shoulders. Now she has sprained her right wrist and is almost immobile. Her sister lives with her and normally helps but is away for a couple of days. Neighbours are kind, but Mrs Snow needs assistance getting to bed at night. It's barely a trained nurses' job, but it needs doing, and there's not a care assistant available. Will you take it on?'

'Of course,' she replied without hesitation. 'It's basic nursing, but it's nursing and, if there's no one else to do it, it's my job, and I'll be only too happy to include Mrs Snow on my list.'

'Thanks. I knew I could count on you.' They smiled at each other across the desk. Like an electric current, vibes of awareness flowed between them, and they were in complete and utter harmony. Their eyes locked together. Imogen held her breath, wanting the magic moment to go on forever.

But of course it couldn't. And Daniel, with a sigh, lowered his eyes and broke the spell. He picked up a batch of patients' notes from his desk, and flicked on the computer screen. He gave Imogen a lopsided grin, and said huskily, 'Work calls. Much as I hate to send you away, I must. I've got to see another patient before starting on my evening calls.' He put his fingers to his lips and kissed them in her direction, and said with a theatrical throb in his voice, 'Parting is such sweet sorrow, as the poet said, but I daren't dally with you longer—you're too much of a distraction. So please go away, woman, and let me get on,' he begged with pretended ferocity.

'All right,' said Imogen in a happy daze, getting up and making for the door. 'I'm on my way to see your precious Mrs Snow and others.'

'Good,' he replied, his eyes twinkling, a quirky smile lifting the corners of his well-marked mouth. He switched on his intercom and spoke into it. 'Mr Greenlough, please, for Dr Granger. . .'

Feeling as if she was walking on air, Imogen returned to the duty-room and gathered together the things she would need for her evening visits, stocking up her case with the necessary dressings, syringes and medication to cover the list of patients she was to see.

Her mind seethed as she worked methodically. Daniel had not spoken of love, but something wonderful had happened between them in his office, something magical, out of this world. . .

She loaded up her car and started on her rounds. Daniel would soon be starting on his. She wondered if she would see him any more this evening. Perhaps when she got back to the centre, he might just possibly be there, waiting for her.

The faint possibility lifted her spirits even further as she drove through the blue and gold of the May evening to her first patient, a Mrs Squire.

Mrs Squire was crippled with arthritis for which she regularly received pain-relieving injections. Normally her husband drove her to the centre for her treatment, but he was at present bed-bound with a virus infection, and Imogen had been asked to give her the injection at home, and check on Mr Squire.

This visit didn't take long. Neither patient needed much attention. She made them both comfortable, wished them a cheerful, 'Goodnight,' and was soon on her way to the next two patients on her list.

The first, a Mr Irving, had been recently discharged from hospital, having had a colostomy performed on the descending colon of his large bowel. The stoma nurse had visited him since his return home and had dealt with the practical side of his problem, showing him how to cope with his colostomy bag and so on, but his wife had requested a visit from someone from the surgery, to 'come and see that things were all right', as she put it.

According to her, the stoma nurse had been efficient. . . 'But you know, Sister,' Mrs Irving tried to explain, nervously patting her greying hair, 'rather brisk. She didn't seem to understand that Jeff's worried about wearing this bag contraption. She may be used to these things, but we're not.'

Imogen spent twenty minutes reassuring the Irvings, leaving them much happier, and promising to visit again.

The second patient, Tracy Pullen, twenty years old,

lived in a squalid room in a large old terraced house that had been turned into bedsits. She had recently been discharged from the local psychiatric hospital, and Dr Strong, who had seen her that morning, had requested a visit by the twilight nurse to confirm that she was taking her medication as prescribed.

She was unwashed, untidy and obviously very unhappy. Her eyes were glazed and vacant. She didn't look well, and made it plain that she didn't want company. At first she refused the tablets prescribed for her, and clearly, left to herself, would not have taken them. It took all of Imogen's persuasive powers to get her to swallow them.

'I'll call again tomorrow,' said Imogen gently but firmly. 'And see how you are.'

Tracy shrugged. 'If you like,' she said.

Imogen drove away from the terrace sad and angry, her thoughts still with Tracy. What a mess the poor girl was in. . .she should still be in care. Perhaps the hospital could be persuaded to take her back, though it didn't seem very likely, as they were trying to clear the unit.

But she had other patients to see and, shrugging off her gloomy thoughts, threaded her way through the evening traffic to the outskirts of the town and Gable End, to see Jonathan.

The first thing she saw as she turned out of the bush-screened drive on to the wide sweep of gravel in front of the house was Daniel's Range Rover, parked outside the front door.

Her heart gave a leap of pleasure at the thought that she would be seeing him again so soon, but she was puzzled as to why he was here. He must have had an emergency call or he would have told her he was visiting the home. But what emergency—surely not

Jonathan? He had been doing so well when she went off duty last week.

Several children, with a couple of adult helpers, were playing on the lawn. Jonathan was not with them. She got out of the car and hurried into the house. There was no one about in the reception hall. Sue, whose office was beside the front door, usually came out to welcome her, but tonight her door remained firmly closed.

It was very quiet except for the sound of children's voices and laughter floating in from the garden.

A sense of foreboding washed over Imogen as she made her way up to the clinic-room on the first floor where she usually saw Jonathan. Something was wrong. It was too quiet. It was a relief to hear voices coming from behind the clinic-room door. She knocked, turned the handle and went in.

Jane Cooper, Sue's chief assistant, Jonathan and his friend Tim were sitting on the floor playing Snakes and Ladders. Imogen let out a sigh of relief. It was quite obvious that Jonathan was all right.

She said, 'It's so quiet here tonight, except for the children in the garden. I thought everyone had run away.'

Jane stood up. 'It's such a lovely evening that they're all outside. Sorry we weren't downstairs to meet you,' she said, 'but, as you see, we got caught up in a fast-moving game.'

Imogen ruffled Jonathan's hair. 'Oh, don't apologise, I'm just glad Jonathan's OK. I saw Daniel's car on the drive and presumed that it was a medical emergency that had brought him out.' She looked enquiringly at Jane.

'Oh, no. It's nothing to do with the children. For some reason Sue wanted to see him urgently about something personal, but I've no idea what. I think that they are still in a huddle in her office. I'm not surprised really; Sue's not been quite herself recently. She and Daniel haven't seen much of each other, not like they used to. I don't know if this has anything to do with tonight's visit by our Dr Dan.' Suddenly she went pink and looked embarrassed. 'And really it's none of my business, so I shouldn't be nattering on like this.'

For some reason Imogen shivered—Daniel and Sue, closeted together. What did it mean? 'It's cold in here,' she said sharply, 'in spite of the sun outside. I think we ought to turn up the heat for the children.'

'It's because it's after the first of May,' explained Jane. 'The heating doesn't come on till later in the evening.'

'Well, it should be on here, in the treatment-room,' Imogen said, still brusque.

'I'll tell Sue,' said Jane quietly, giving Imogen a surprised look.

'Please do. Now I'd better see to Jonathan.' She was cool and professional.

'Of course,' said Jane pleasantly.

At once Imogen felt ashamed of herself for being so stiff and unfriendly with poor Jane. She knew that she had suddenly felt prickly and irritable because Jane had referred to Daniel and Sue as an item. Well, she had to face it, maybe they were. Perhaps the rumours that she'd heard about them had been true all the time, and she had read too much into Daniel's manner towards her and his invitation to dinner. Maybe he was just being protective, caring, because he was that sort of man. Ridiculous—she hadn't imagined what had happened in his office this evening; that had been real enough.

She was confused, unhappy, but she didn't have to

take it out on Jane. Impulsively she put out her hand and touched the young housemother's arm. 'I'm so sorry,' she said, 'to have been so beastly to you. It's silly to make a fuss about the heating; it's just me, I'm afraid, I felt shivery. I think I may have a cold coming.'

Jane accepted her explanation and was immediately sympathetic. 'You poor thing, I hope it's not one last gasp of the tummy bug. Would you like tea or coffee before you see to Jonathan? That might make you feel better.'

'No, thanks, I'll get on. I've loads more patients to see.'

Suddenly Imogen wanted to be out of the house and be gone before Daniel knew that she had been there; she couldn't face a confrontation now. She had almost convinced herself that Daniel and Sue were just good friends, but she doubted if Sue felt the same. She had no idea why Sue had wanted to see Daniel this evening, but if it was personal, as Jane suspected, it had to be something to do with their relationship with each other. Perhaps Sue suspects there is something going on between Daniel and me, she thought, and wants to get the situation cleared up. It is what I should do in her place. I would rather know the truth than go on hoping in vain.

Forcing herself to put aside these vague, unsubstantiated reasons for Daniel's being closeted with Sue, she concentrated on taking Jonathan's blood sample, giving him his injection of insulin and filling in his chart, while listening to his happy chatter. What a change there was in the boy since he had first come to Gable End, and it was all down to Sue and her staff and their expertise and loving care. He had made friends of his own accord and was settling down in school happily, as Sue had forecast. What a wonderful person she was. How sad if she had to be hurt because Daniel had fallen out of love with her, if indeed that was true.

Impatiently Imogen squashed her unhelpful thoughts, wished the boys goodnight and gathered up her case. Jane accompanied her out on to the balcony overlooking the hall. 'You should go home,' she said in a concerned voice, 'and have a hot drink and some aspirin to stop that cold, or whatever it is, getting any worse. You look quite pale, not your usual self at all.'

'I'm all right,' insisted Imogen. 'You get back to the kids and your scintillating game of Snakes and Ladders.' She raised a smile.

'OK, if you're sure. Goodnight, Imogen; see you.'

'See you,' replied Imogen.

She was about to go downstairs when a door opened in the hall below. Peering over the banisters, she saw Daniel and Sue emerge from Sue's office. Daniel had an arm round Sue's shoulders, and she had an arm round his waist and was smiling up at him. She said something to him and he laughed and bent his head down to kiss her.

Imogen froze. She couldn't believe what she was seeing. Only an hour or so earlier Daniel had been tender and loving with her, yet here he was kissing Sue Forsythe. And a moment ago she had been worried about Sue being hurt! How ludicrous. Her heart felt like a stone in her chest.

On a rising tide of panic, she wondered what she should do. Ideas raced through her mind. Should she go down and confront them? Stay where she was and hope they wouldn't realise that she was in the house? That wouldn't do—they would see her car parked on the drive. Would Daniel seek her out, and tell her the truth about his feelings for Sue, or would he try to bluff it out and still pretend that they were only good friends?

His actions didn't make any sense. She couldn't believe that he was the philandering sort. He wouldn't string two women along at the same time, would he? And yet she had seen him kiss Sue moments before, and they were still standing there now in the middle of the hall, arms about each other, talking in low voices—the way lovers might.

It couldn't be happening. . .it had to be a bad dream.

There was a sudden clattering of feet on the front porch and a clamour of young voices as a crowd of youngsters came pouring into the hall from the garden.

Sue and Daniel drew apart, and turned to welcome the tide of children. Daniel scooped up a little girl and sat her on his shoulders, and the child squealed with delight. 'Where are we going?' Imogen heard him ask.

'Going to supper,' the small girl shrieked.

Sue was smiling down at the huddle of children around her, all excitedly telling her about their game. She began shepherding them towards the back corridor beneath the balcony, where the kitchen and dining-room were located, and, as suddenly as it had filled, the hall emptied.

For a moment Imogen didn't move. She couldn't believe her luck; she would be able to leave without Daniel and Sue being any the wiser. She tore down the stairs and across to the front door, and had her hand on the latch, when Daniel spoke from the back of the hall, a note of surprise in his voice. 'Imogen, what on earth are you rushing off for? I thought and hoped, as you must have seen my car, that you'd be coming to find me before you left. I saw you arrive when I was in Sue's office.'

She said, in a soft, tremulous, but venomous voice, her fury barely contained, 'Don't pretend, Daniel, not any more; there's no need, I saw you with Sue, just now in the hall, kissing her.'

Daniel looked startled, but not embarrassed. 'Did you—where on earth were you hiding?'

At once the emphasis was turned around; he made it seem as if she had been spying on him.

'I wasn't exactly hiding. I was just about to come down the stairs.'

'Well, why on earth didn't you come all the way down?'

'Because I didn't think you'd want to see me at that point.'

'What point?' he asked sharply.

'When you were kissing Sue.'

'For heaven's sake, one can kiss a friend, surely, without arousing suspicion?' He crossed the hall, put out a hand and lifted Imogen's chin, so that her eyes were forced to meet his. 'Or were you suspicious?' He looked hard into her eyes. 'By God,' he said angrily, 'you were.' He let go her chin and took a step backwards. 'You thought that I was capable of making love to Sue after what happened between us in my office this evening! I don't believe it. . .you couldn't think that badly of me.'

'I didn't know what to think, and I still don't. You always look so close, you and Sue. It's hard to believe that there isn't more than just friendship between you.'

'You'd better believe it, my dear Imogen,' he said flatly in a voice full of suppressed rage. 'We're old and good friends and will remain that way forever. And as an old friend, Sue wanted me to be the first to know her good news, that she had got the job that she was hankering after. It's been in the balance for the last few weeks, and she was feeling down in the dumps about it, quite unlike her usual confident self.'

Suddenly everything that Jane had said about Sue's being despondent clicked into place. Except that it wasn't Daniel who had caused her depression, but the uncertainty about the job, whatever that was. Imogen's heart lifted a notch or two.

'Is it very important, the job?' she asked faintly.

'To Sue it is. It's all she ever wanted, to start up a children's home from scratch. And now that's what she's been offered down in the West Country. A free hand. A shell of a building and acres of land to do with as she thinks fit. To provide the very best care for disadvantaged children. It's a trust foundation with, for once, ample funding behind it. Sue's a career person through and through—there can be no compromise with her.'

'And you're pleased for her?'

'Naturally—it's what she's always wanted.'

'The fact that she is a career person hasn't anything to do with why you and she aren't. . .?' Her voice petered out at the sight of Daniel's stony look.

'Married, engaged, having an affair, and at the same time flirting with you? Is that what you're asking, Imogen?' he said silkily.

'Yes, I suppose I am,' she muttered miserably.

'And you're thinking that you are perhaps second best and I've turned to you because Sue's not available, is that what you think?'

'Well. . .' She felt sick with misery. The conversation was going all wrong. He was clearly innocent of all the sins she had mentally accused him of. She sounded nagging and suspicious, when all she wanted was a reassurance that he respected, perhaps even loved her. But could he love or respect her after this?

She swallowed her pride and all her other treacherous emotions and said softly, praying that he would understand, 'Will you forgive me for not seeming to trust you? I was terribly muddled and the sort of friendship that you two have is unusual. . .I think I was jealous.'

'Does that mean that you still want us to pursue *our* friendship?'

'With all my heart,' she whispered, her eyes meeting his unwaveringly.

Daniel looked at her steadily for a moment. Then his face softened. He said quietly, 'In that case, Imogen, love, I forgive you.' He held his arms wide. 'Now come here and let me kiss you,' he commanded.

She went into his arms and raised her face to his, and caught a wisp of cologne as slowly he lowered his head. She was conscious that his firm, well-marked mouth looked startlingly red against the shadowy stubble of his chin. He looked incredibly sexy and passionate. Holding her breath, she waited, expecting a long and intimate kiss, but to her surprise, the kiss when it came on her slightly parted lips was brief, cool and deliberate. And after only a moment he raised his head. 'That,' he said in a low voice, 'is just to be going on with, something on account, as it were, but there'll be more to follow at a later date, and it'll be the real thing then, no holding back. I'm mad for you, Imogen.' His mouth quirked into a smile. 'But now is not the time or place for me to tell you how *much* I want you; that must wait. We'd better go before we're knee-deep in the children coming out from their supper. And anyway, as always, we both have work to do.'

Imogen swallowed her disappointment at the coolness of his kiss. 'My goodness, yes,' she said calmly, checking her watch. 'I must fly.'

'Right.' Daniel planted another quick, matter-of-fact

kiss on her forehead, opened the door, ushered her through in front of him and escorted her to her car. 'Drive carefully,' he said softly as she fastened her seat-belt.

She nodded slowly as she looked up into his face, its rugged bone-structure bathed in the mellow evening sunlight, all strong masculine planes and firm angles. She loved every inch of it. His eyes were very green. It didn't matter about the kiss being cool—he was right: it wasn't the time or place to be anything else.

It was all happening, she felt. It had been inevitable since their first meeting, this drawing together. Her pulses raced as, outwardly calm, inwardly absurdly happy, she switched on the ignition, put the car into gear, released the handbrake and started to move off. In her rear mirror she could see him standing watching as she pulled away. And he was still standing there motionless when she turned the corner into the bush-sheltered drive.

It was some ten minutes later before some tiny doubts began to prick at her happiness.

She drew up outside her next patient's house and sat staring into space for a few minutes, deep in thought.

There had been magic moments between her and Daniel ever since they had first met, and she had been steadily falling in love with him for weeks. Of course, *he* had never actually said that he was in love with *her*, but he had intimated as much. And he had made it plain this evening that he wanted to make love to her, and soon. It was inevitable that their relationship would grow stronger, closer, permanent.

A permanent relationship! Marriage! It was an enormous step to take. Much as she loved him, was she ready to take it? Ready to give up her commitment to Aunt Sophie and the family? She couldn't let them down. They were all so vulnerable at the moment. Could she count on his forbearance while she sorted out her feelings and her obligations? He was a patient, gentle and understanding doctor, but would he be the same on a personal level?

Yes, her instinct told her, he would. He was as kind and considerate as a man as he was a doctor. However much he wanted them to be together, surely he wouldn't expect her to reject her responsibilities, would give her time? Nevertheless, as she walked up the path to the patient's house she felt a slight twinge of doubt, enough to take the fine edge off what should have been undiluted happiness.

Training and practice came to her aid as she knocked at the door and waited to be admitted to the neat semi-detached house to attend a Mr Loder. Patients first, as Daniel had said, and for the rest of the evening she concentrated all her care and expertise on them, and pushed aside her own mixed emotions to deal with in her own time.

The elderly Mr Loder, who was making a slow recovery from a severe attack of flu which had left him shaky and housebound, had an abscess on the back of his neck, known as a collar stud abscess. It had been surgically incised a few days earlier, and a drain had been inserted to allow the pus to escape. It was a painful condition, and the skin around the affected area was red, tender and warm.

He looked at Imogen apprehensively. 'It isn't going to hurt, is it? I seem to have lost all my bottle these days; can't stand a bit of pain.'

'I'll be as gentle as I can,' she reassured him. 'I'm going to remove the dirty dressing, swab the wound and the drain with a special cleaning agent and put on a new dressing, that's all. It won't take me long, and then I'll give you your antibiotic injection, and you'll be comfortable for the night.'

Some time later she left Mr Loder a much happier man, his rheumy blue eyes twinkling naughtily. 'You've certainly got a gentle touch, Sister, and you're pretty with it. You can come and see me any time,' he said almost roguishly as he insisted on seeing her to the door.

His approval cheered her immensely, and by the end of the evening visits her earlier euphoria was more or less in place. She and Daniel would come together somehow; that was all that mattered. They would iron out any difficulties that arose. Nothing was insurmountable.

On this note, tired and mostly reassured, Imogen went home to bed, and fell asleep directly her head touched the pillow.

CHAPTER EIGHT

THE following morning, just after she had given the twins their breakfast and seen them off to school, the phone rang; and because he was filling her thoughts Imogen knew before she lifted the receiver that it was Daniel ringing. Her heart bumped with pleasure in anticipation of hearing his voice. What would he have to say to her after all that had happened yesterday? There had been the tender interlude in his office, their meeting and parting at Gable End. Perhaps he would be warm, loving, passionate even.

She wished him a rather breathless, 'Good morning.'

His reply was brisk. Not warm, loving or passionate but brusque and businesslike.

'Morning, Imogen,' he said crisply, 'This is just a brief call. There's a roomful of people waiting to see me. But I just wanted to let you know that I've wangled some time off on Saturday, so I'm taking you out to dinner for our long-deferred date. I'll call for you at about seven-thirty.'

Imogen was taken aback by his abruptness. It was as if yesterday had never happened—there was no tenderness, no gentleness in his voice, just an assumption that she would fall in with his plans. He might have been giving her instructions about a patient.

She took a deep breath, and said coolly, 'I'm afraid that won't be possible, Daniel; I'm working on Saturday.'

'No, you're not—I've arranged for someone to cover for you,' he said flatly.

'What?' The word exploded angrily from her. The effrontery of the man! This was the second time he had presumed to make arrangements for her without consulting her. How incredibly arrogant and high-handed. . .and to do it in such a manner, such a tone, with no attempt to be persuasive! He had issued his invitation almost like an order. Well, no way was she going to allow him to take her for granted. She was shaking with anger, but she made her voice steady, and said icily, 'And supposing I don't want to go out to dinner with you on Saturday, Daniel?'

There was a moment's silence, and then he said, his voice infuriatingly mild and reasonable. 'My dear Imogen, the thought never entered my head. I presumed that you would want to see me as much as I want to see you, especially after last night. Am I wrong about that?'

So he had remembered last night and their parting at Gable End. Her anger subsided a little.

Her mind raced as she reviewed his words and actions. When it came down to it, he had done nothing wrong; he had simply made it possible for them to see each other, something they had been trying to do for weeks. So he had been high-handed, forceful about it. He had assumed that she wanted to see him. Well, she did. So why not admit it? Why not for once let someone else make decisions? Why not be feminine and helpless? Used as she was to fending for herself, and latterly doing most of the thinking for the Jackson household, why not relax and have decisions made for her by a capable man who cared, as Daniel seemed to care?

Traitorously, a warm glow replaced her anger. She said softly, 'Of course you're not wrong, Daniel. I want to go out to dinner with you.'

'Good. I'm glad about that,' he said drily. 'Goodbye, love. Take care. I might see you this evening. . .not sure; I'm doing William's calls as well as my own. I look forward to Saturday.'

He rang off.

'And so do I,' she murmured as she replaced the receiver.

When she went on duty that evening, she learned that Daniel had already left on his evening visits. She suppressed her disappointment, tried to put him out of her mind and got on with checking her own list of patients she had to see. It was going to be another busy session.

The phone rang just as she was going out of the door. 'Imogen,' said Felicity Collins, the one woman doctor at the centre. 'Can you possibly fit in another visit for me? I know it's a late request, but I've just had an SOS from a Mrs Allen in Church Street. I wouldn't ask you if it wasn't urgent.'

Imogen had a soft spot for Felicity. She was a good doctor, and, because she was the only woman, took on more than her fair share of maternity and paediatric cases. She seldom asked favours. She said cheerfully, 'If I can I will. What's the problem?'

'A cystic fibrosis infant, name of Simon. Mrs Allen has three children under five. Her husband's a long-distance lorry driver. When he's away, Mrs Allen's mother usually visits to help with the evening chores, seeing to the other children while their mother gives Simon his physio, which she's been taught in hospital. Apparently Mum's ill, a friend and neighbour away, and Mrs Allen's on her own and can't cope.'

'I'm not surprised,' said Imogen drily. 'I don't think I could cope with three under-fives, especially if one of them's ill. What do you want me to do, Felicity?'

'Give Simon his treatment while Mrs Allen sees to the other two. I know you've had some experience in this field.'

'I know the basic physiotherapy, so I'm happy to give it a go. I'll put the Allen family top of my list.'

'Many thanks. I'm most grateful.'

It had been raining all day, but the rain had stopped, though the sky was still iron-grey, when Imogen knocked at the door of number eleven Church Street.

The door was opened by a thin, tired-looking young woman with a small boy straddling her hip and accompanied by two pretty red-headed but tearful little girls clinging to her skirts. 'Oh, Sister,' she exclaimed, 'am I glad to see you! Dr Collins said you would come. I don't know which way to turn. The girls haven't had their supper or their baths, and they're tired and hungry, and Simon needs his physio—if he doesn't have it, his chest fills up. Can you help?'

'That's what I'm here for,' said Imogen reassuringly as she followed Mrs Allen down the narrow hall. 'Now, if Simon will come to me, I'll see to him while you give the girls their supper and so on.' She smiled at the three children, who were all staring at her with wide eyes. After a moment they smiled tremulously back at her. She held out her arms to Simon, and rather to her surprise he allowed his mother to hand him over without a murmur. 'Well, you are a good boy,' she said softly, dropping a kiss on his auburn curls.

'He's been in hospital so much since he was born that he's used to nurses in uniform,' explained Mrs Allen.

And, young as he was, the two-and-a-half-year-old Simon seemed to know his routine. To Imogen's amazement he co-operated with her as she pummelled his small chest and back and put him through the rest of his exercises, until he had coughed up a quantity of thick, sticky mucous.

By the time she had finished and handed Simon over to his mother, the girls had been bathed and fed and were happily watching a cartoon on television in the small front sitting-room.

'Do stay and have a coffee, Sister,' invited Mrs Allen, tucking her son in between the girls on the sofa, and giving him a biscuit to nibble at. 'I'd appreciate some adult conversation, as I've only had the kids to talk to all day. I love them like mad, but they can get a bit wearing, to say the least. I've missed having my mum here today, and my neighbour's away. Please say you'll stay just for a few minutes.'

Pressed as she was, no way could Imogen bring herself to refuse; the young woman badly needed some company, and it was all part of twilight nursing. 'All right,' she agreed, 'but it *will* only be for a few minutes, as I've lots of other patients to see.'

Some ten minutes later Imogen drove away from Church Street, with Mrs Allen's grateful thanks ringing in her ears. Wouldn't it be brilliant, she mused, if some of the active, older people in the town, perhaps recently retired, itching to do something useful, could get together with people in need of support like Mrs Allen? Be a sort of substitute mum or good neighbour?

Was it just a fanciful idea, or was there some substance in it? Could, for instance, the twilight nursing service be extended to include voluntary lay helpers, people who had time to chat to the Mrs Allens of this world, or read to the kids while Mum washed her hair? Small, practical things outside the scope of the nurses or care assistants? Of course, it would need careful planning. A register of helpers would have to be drawn up and vetted.

Would the health-centre doctors support the idea? Would Daniel back her up? If he did, she felt that the other doctors would do so.

It was an interesting proposition which continued to occupy her until she reached Arundel Road, where she was to visit, for the first time, an Ian Lundy.

She didn't relish this call. According to the notes she had been given, Ian, of below-average intelligence, was dying of cancer, but had discharged himself from the hospice a couple of days before. He was in his thirties and was being nursed by his elderly parents. He had refused to see any of the hospice visiting nurses, so the chore of giving him his pain-killing injections and lending support to the family had devolved on the health-centre staff. It looked like being another lengthy visit.

In the event, she was not in the house very long. Ian's favourite sister had arrived and was giving much-needed moral support to him and to their parents. Imogen had nothing to do except to give him his injection, and check his vulnerable pressure areas.

In no time at all she was on her way to her next patient. The rest of the evening went smoothly. She gave more injections, renewed dressings, doled out night medication as necessary and, of course, gave constant reassurance.

By ten o'clock she was on her way home.

Tired but happy after a successful evening's work, she went to bed and dreamed of Daniel, Mrs Allen, and a host of small red-headed children with their arms outstretched in supplication. But by morning she had only vague, tantalising memories of the dream.

* * *

Over the next few days she and Daniel saw little of each other. They met occasionally when she came on duty, but they were both busy and there were always other people around. The most they could do was to smile into each other's eyes, perhaps touch hands, and long for Saturday to come.

The weekend came at last, and, having decided that she had nothing suitable to wear for her dinner date with Daniel, Imogen took herself into the centre of town to one of the smart little boutiques that abounded.

She had the sort of figure that was easy to fit, slender with small, high breasts, and long shapely legs. She was spoilt for choice and she decided that she would be extravagant for once and buy exactly what she wanted.

After trying on an endless number of dresses, skirts, tunics and separates she settled on a baggy pure silk blouse—with a plunging neckline, flower splashed, in muted shades of blue and violet which matched her eyes and contrasted with the rich chestnut of her hair—over purple velvet stirrup pants. The long, loose, richly floating silk blouse was deceptively modest, but, combined with the close-fitting pants hugging her long, curvy legs, produced a very sexy effect. An effect, she acknowledged, that she was deliberately aiming at to remove any doubts in Daniel's mind that she was a man-hating feminist, of which he had once teasingly accused her. Pink strappy sandals and a pink velvet clutch bag completed her ensemble, and, much poorer but happy, Imogen left the boutique and returned home.

The house was very quiet, the twins out to a birthday party of one of their schoolfellows, and Imogen was in her room putting the finishing touches to her make-up, when the side doorbell rang.

She heard Laurie go down to answer it, and a few minutes later she heard his voice and Daniel's deeper one in conversation as they mounted the stairs.

She couldn't believe how wildly her heart thumped and her hand trembled at the sound of Daniel's voice. It was ridiculous. She felt that it should be happening to someone else, not to her. She longed to rush out and meet him, but made herself stay put in front of her dressing-table, putting further unnecessary touches to her make-up.

After a little while her pulse returned more or less to normal, and she felt that she could meet him without giving herself away. She draped her midnight-blue cashmere shawl in soft folds round her shoulders, gathered up her clutch bag, and made for the sitting-room.

Daniel was sitting beside Aunt Sophie at the far end of the long, elegant room that ran the length of the front of the house, above the shop, the storerooms and office. He stood up as she entered, tall and lean and incredibly masculine in a traditional, beautifully tailored black evening suit with a plain white starched shirt. He moved swiftly down the room and took both her hands in his. His dark hair gleamed, his firm chin, though obviously recently shaved, showed the faintest shadow of a beard, emphasising its strong squareness. He was aggressively masculine. His amused hazel eyes swept over her appreciatively, and she was glad that she had invested in the expensive designer outfit that looked and felt just right.

He squeezed her fingers. 'Imogen, you look wonderful,' he said in a low voice. 'So soft, so utterly feminine, so unfeminist, if there is such a word. Do you forgive me for ever even suggesting otherwise?'

She nodded and smiled wryly. 'Of course; I was sure that you couldn't mean it.' A whisper of a tremor ran up her arms at the touch of his fingers. She did her best to ignore it, but she couldn't ignore the warmth emanating from him, which seemed to draw her closer, like a magnet. His smiling eyes devoured her and she felt herself drowning in them. Somehow, exerting all her powers of self-control, she added in a cool, detached voice, 'And I'm glad that you recognise true femininity when you see it.' She gave a small laugh as she lowered her eyes and broke contact with him, withdrawing her hands from his.

Laurie called loudly, in a half-cross, half-teasing manner, 'Do we get a chance to look at this gorgeous female, Daniel, or are you going to hog her to yourself? After all, you've got her for the rest of the evening.'

'Yes,' said Aunt Sophie. 'Come over here, Imogen, and let us see what you look like in your lovely new outfit. Remember, you promised me a little fashion show.'

'A new outfit,' said Daniel quietly, though his eyes gleamed wickedly, 'just for me?'

'Certainly not,' said Imogen, returning his smile as they walked the length of the long, low room. 'I dress to please myself.'

'Really?' said Daniel with a quiet chuckle. 'I just don't believe that.'

He was right, of course, mused Imogen as a short while later they drove out of the town, she had dressed to please and intrigue him, and he knew it.

They turned west, facing into the low, brilliant light of the setting sun. In the confines of the car, she breathed in sharply, very conscious of his closeness. His aftershave wafted over in little waves each time he turned his head.

'All right?' he asked, briefly covering her tightly

clasped hands with one of his. 'You seem rather tense. There's nothing wrong, is there?'

She shook her head. 'No, I'm fine thank you. It's a lovely evening.'

'Perfect.' He flashed her another fleeting smile and she knew that he was not just referring to the sunset and the weather.

Surprisingly, after that exchange, the small silence that settled between them was a comfortable one. Her eyes were drawn to his lean, strong hands with their scattering of dark hairs, resting in a relaxed position on the steering-wheel. What beautiful hands, she thought. He was an excellent driver, overtaking smoothly when he was able, or staying, without visible signs of frustration, behind slower vehicles when conditions demanded.

'We're going to Abbots,' he said. 'Do you know it?'

'No, but I've heard of it. Aunt Sophie used to go there often. According to her, it's rather gracious and old world.'

'It is. I love it. After the day-to-day hassle of modern medicine, I find it wonderfully relaxing.'

Imogen was surprised. 'I wouldn't have thought that you were bothered by the day-to-day hassle; you always seem so unruffled.'

'That makes me sound almost indifferent.'

'Oh, no, not at all. Please, I don't think that.' She was anxious that he shouldn't misunderstand her. Unselfconsciously she put a hand on his arm for a moment. 'You are a very caring doctor—everyone says so and I've seen it for myself, and especially with the children at Gable End. I just meant that you seem to ooze calm and self-confidence. It's hard to think of you as feeling bothered.'

He looked sideways at her, and said, his voice serious, 'I might say the same about you, as you always emanate a queenly calm. Surely all of us in medicine and nursing acquire a veneer? We need it.' Before she could answer he added matter-of-factly, 'Well, here we are—we've arrived,' and turned off the main road into what was obviously a long, winding drive between trees and shrubs.

Abbots, the superb, elegant hotel converted from a pre-Elizabethan monastery, lay in the heart of the Sussex weald surrounded by trees. Daniel got a warm greeting from the *maître d'*, marking him out as a regular visitor. Imogen looked around with interest as they were escorted to a discreetly furnished sitting area, with richly plush armchairs and polished low tables, to have drinks and hors-d'oeuvres while they waited for their dinner.

They both chose to drink small dry Martinis with lots of ice.

'Well, that's one little thing that I've learned about you at last,' said Daniel, leaning back in his comfortable armchair, long legs stretched out before him, and twiddling his cocktail glass, 'you like dry Martinis.'

'My favourite drink,' said Imogen. 'Is it yours?'

'No, a good malt whisky is my preference, but I'm being abstemious as I'm driving. I shall have half a glass of wine with dinner, but nothing more.'

'I'm glad to hear it. We see enough in our line of work to condemn drinking and driving.' She regretted what she had said, even as she said it, for they would be trapped in shop talk.

'That's a fact; we're certainly at the sharp end.'

'By the way, the accident the other week. . .have you heard anything? What with the tummy-bug epidemic and everything, I lost track of how they got on. I wondered if the driver of the car that hit the boy had been drinking. He didn't come from the pub on the green, and the child did dash into the road, so it wasn't entirely his fault.'

'Well, apparently he was over the limit, but whether that had anything to do with the accident I wouldn't know, though it probably slowed his reflex actions down. He might have been able to stop had he been less the worse for drink. I phoned the hospital and spoke to a friend of mine there. The bloke had a whiplash injury to his spine. A good job you told the chap who went to his aid to keep him as still as possible, as it certainly prevented more damage occurring.'

'And what about the boy?'

'He had a hairline skull fracture, but should do OK with care and treatment.'

'Poor kid, but at least he survived the accident—so many don't.'

Daniel looked at her under half-lowered lashes partly veiling his teasing hazel eyes as he lounged back in the armchair. 'Probably thanks to you and your first aiding, Imogen. The wrong move at the wrong time might have caused all sorts of complications. You responded splendidly at the accident.'

'I didn't feel so splendid. I'd like to brush up on my first-aid work.' She took a sip of her drink, and an idea came to her. 'Daniel, couldn't we have a refresher course or something at the health centre, with you or one of the other doctors instructing?'

Daniel sat up straight in his chair, and looked at her thoughtfully. 'You know,' he said, 'that's not a bad idea. All the staff could attend, and perhaps even patients who are interested. But we ought to get one of the paramedics or attached emergency medicos to instruct us. They're the real experts in this field. We GPs get out of date.'

They stared at each other, intrigued by the idea. A waiter materialised beside Daniel.

'Your table is ready, sir,' he announced.

'Right,' said Daniel. He placed his still half-full glass of Martini on the table, stood up in one easy movement and held out both his hands. 'Come, Imogen,' he said, and his eyes, meeting hers, were a mixture of laughter and tenderness. 'Let's go and eat—I'm starving.'

She put down her glass and placed both her hands in his, and he pulled her to her feet. The waiter had gone ahead and for a moment they had the little sitting-room to themselves. The atmosphere changed—suddenly it was crackling with pent-up emotion. Daniel pulled her close to him until she fancied she could feel the steady throb of his heart against her breast through the thin silk of her blouse. She said, 'Oh, Daniel,' in a muffled whisper, and looked up into his strong but gentle face.

He brushed his lips across hers. 'You're lovely,' he said in a soft, husky voice. 'No more shop talk. I want to talk about you. I want to know all there is to know about you, from the day you were born till now. I've waited so long to get to know you.'

'But we've only known each other for a short while,' she said on a bubble of laughter, trying desperately to be casual, but dizzy with happiness, hardly able to believe that she was standing crushed against his shirt-front.

'It seems like forever since I met you in the supermarket and thought you were unobtainable; a young mum with a hungry family to feed.'

'I thought you were unobtainable too.'

'Why, for heaven's sake?'

'Because——' A discreet cough from the waiter in the doorway prevented her from answering. 'I'll tell you some time,' she said breathlessly.

'Promise?'

'Promise.'

He nodded, collected her wrap and bag from the armchair, put a warm hand beneath her elbow, and, following the waiter, escorted her to the dining-room.

Their table, laid with a snow-white cloth, sparkling glasses and heavy cutlery, was in a plant-screened windowed alcove overlooking the parkland and lake. Lights from the wide terrace mirrored themselves in the water, and a rising moon silvered the rippling surface.

It was beautiful, an invitation to romance. Not, thought Imogen as with a fast-beating heart, and aware of his eyes upon her, she took her place opposite to Daniel at the sumptuous table, that we need any encouragement.

As soon as the waiter had left them to choose their food, Daniel stretched across the table, removed Imogen's elegant menu card from her nerveless fingers, and wrapped his hands round hers. His warm hazel eyes looked deep into her violet-blue ones. 'Imogen,' he whispered huskily, 'I'm fast falling in love with you. . .in fact I think I fell in love with you on the day that we met, three times over.'

'Three times?'

'First when you bumped into me with your laden trolley, and you apologised so nicely, and looked so *distraite*. Second when you appeared in the car park with the rain pouring down your face and your fringe plastered to your forehead. . .' He paused.

'And third?' she prompted.

'When I entered your godmother's bookshop, and found you perched on a ladder, and you explained who you were, and my heart lifted, because I knew that you weren't committed to a husband and babies.'

'Oh,' Imogen murmured, her heart pumping madly. 'But I have got a commitment, you know, to Aunt Sophie and Laurie and the twins—they need me.'

'But it's only temporary; you're not committed for life, are you?' He frowned. 'There's never been anything serious between you and Laurie, has there?'

Imogen shook her head. 'Not on my side, no.'

'On his?'

'I think he fancied there was. He's missing his wife, Daniel, and the children are missing their mother, as you know. It's not surprising that he's trying to fill the void.'

A strange expression flitted across Daniels' face. He pressed her captured fingers. 'That's the trouble,' he growled. 'Laurie's trying to get through to your generous, loving heart, Imogen, with a kind of emotional blackmail; it gives him an advantage.'

'Not over me it doesn't. Of course I feel desperately sorry for him, and I'm fond of him and the children, but I know where to draw the line between caring and. . .'

'And?' His eyes were brilliant as they bored into hers, his hands tightening round her fingers.

'And anything more serious,' she whispered, wishing that she had the courage to say 'loving', which was what she was sure he wanted to hear.

They looked long and hard into each other's eyes and exchanged all sorts of subtle messages. Imogen tingled all over, hardly daring to breathe, hardly daring to believe what was happening to her. Daniel was telling her with his eyes that he wanted her with a passion too deep for words. She was almost frightened by the intensity she saw there, and, trembling, she tried to pull her hands from his, but with the slightest extra pressure he continued to hold them.

After what seemed an eternity when everything stood still, and sounds became muted and then vanished, he spoke. 'Don't fight it, Imogen; it's inevitable. . .we've been attracted from the start. And don't be frightened; I wouldn't do anything to hurt you.' His voice was low and husky and his eyes still blazed, but with a gentler passion now.

Imogen almost stopped breathing. Daniel was telling her that he wanted to make love to her. And she wanted him to—she had never been so sure of anything in her life. She had never felt like this before about any man, and she was practised at warding off unwelcome advances. But his advances wouldn't be unwelcome. She wanted to surrender to him. Her thoughts rioted. She longed to feel his arms about her, and his body pressed close and into hers in the ultimate delight and feel his wonderful, lean hands exploring her naked body. She shivered and blushed at her wild thoughts, and jerked herself out of her reverie. But she knew, without a doubt, that if, at the end of the evening, he wanted to make love to her she would let him.

Her decision made her feel all at once confident and relaxed. Her blush subsided. She gave him a happy smile, and said softly, 'Oh, I'm not frightened, Daniel, not of you. I know I can trust you implicitly.'

Daniel said, 'My darling girl, that's the nicest thing you could possibly say to me.'

There was another discreet cough from the waiter, who had reappeared at the end of the table. 'Are you ready to order, sir, or shall I come back?' he asked.

Daniel loosened his hold on Imogen's hands and picked up his menu, giving her a wry smile as he did so. 'Shall I,' he asked, indicating the menu, 'order for both of us?'

'Please.' Her voice was a little unsteady, her heart hammering away in the region of her throat. She wanted to say that she wasn't really hungry any more, but of course that just wasn't possible—the social niceties had to be observed.

'Any particular likes or dislikes?'

'I won't eat veal and I'd prefer fish as a main course.'

'Then a simple starter, say avocado vinaigrette, followed by fillets of sole cooked to the chef's special recipe and served with creamed spinach, small new potatoes and *petits pois*. And to finish, *crème brûlée* such as you've never tasted before.'

'Sounds a feast to remember.'

'Oh, it will be,' he said, smiling into her eyes, 'for more reasons than one.'

The wine waiter came, and Daniel ordered a half-bottle of what she guessed was very good champagne. 'Since I'm only having a splash,' he explained, 'it'll be up to you to finish the bottle.'

Imogen chuckled. 'Are you trying to get me tipsy, by any chance?' she asked. 'I do believe that your intentions are dishonourable, sir.'

'Oh, they are,' he said with a laugh, 'strictly dishonourable.'

CHAPTER NINE

DINNER was memorable, as Daniel promised it would be. Though simple, the food was superbly cooked and presented, and the service discreet. There was a magic about everything. Imogen felt lightheaded with happiness and was conscious of Daniel's presence all the time. Beneath the table their feet and ankles occasionally touched, sending tingling waves of awareness trembling through her body.

They longed to be alone, to talk intimately, but as the waiters came and went they tried to make casual conversation. It was after their coffee was served that Daniel said softly, 'Now tell me all there is to know about yourself, Imogen, everything.' His eyes were teasing and warm. 'Life story—I want to learn every fascinating detail there is to know about you.'

Imogen laughed. 'Fascinating! Oh, Daniel, my life's been very dull.'

'My dear girl,' he said, his voice serious, 'nothing about you is dull for me.' Their eyes locked on to each other for a moment, and she felt herself prickle with delight. 'Now please tell all.'

He was a good listener, and she found herself pouring out the story of her happy childhood enjoyed against a stable background of loving parents. 'Which was why,' she explained sadly, 'it was so traumatic when my parents separated when I was sixteen. It came as an awful shock to me, though apparently they had been unhappy for a long time, and had only stayed together for my sake, because they loved me very much, and still do. I don't know how they kept up the fiction. Since then, they've both remarried, and I'm welcome in both their homes, but it's not the same as a family home, of seeing them both together.'

'And that's where your godmother comes into the picture,' said Daniel gently.

'Yes, Aunt Sophie was marvellous; she gave me a home and love and support when my parents split up, which is why I'm happy to help her and Laurie and the children now. Especially the children, because their parents have separated, as mine did, and it's worse for them because they are younger. I want do to for them what Aunt Sophie did for me.'

'Provide a mother figure? Yes, I can understand that,' Daniel said quietly.

'Can you?' she asked sceptically. 'I wonder? It's something you have to experience, to understand the utter loneliness and confusion a child feels at being separated from a parent. I know you're sympathetic, but you've had a constant and loving relationship with your parents, so it's impossible for you to understand what it's like to be a child without a mother.'

Daniel smiled wryly. 'Well, actually,' he said in a quiet, unemotional voice, 'it's not. I understand only too well, because I was an unwanted baby. I spent several years in foster or children's homes as a child. I never knew what a real home was until I was adopted by the most loving people in the world, and brought up as their son.'

'Oh, Daniel!' Imogen felt herself go pale with shock. Her hand crept across the table and found his, and their fingers laced together. 'I had no idea.' She blinked back tears as she looked at him. 'Tell me about it.'

'Well, that's it really. I wasn't adopted as a baby,

because I was not a very well child. My dear adoptive parents appeared when I was five years old, and decided to take me on. I spent weekends with them, and after the lengthy process demanded by law, was eventually adopted by them. Dad was a busy GP in the east end of London, Mother had been a nurse at Guy's until they married. I took to the idea of medicine like a duck to water, and began to grow and thrive in the atmosphere of love and interest that they gave me. I've never looked back, I am as you see me now, and I owe everything to them, Imogen, everything. Like your godmother, they're wonderful people, and I would do anything for them.'

'Of course you would, so you do understand that I feel the same about Aunt Sophie, and Laurie and the twins. . .I would simply do anything for them.'

'Yes, well that's natural, but keep a sense of proportion, Imogen; remember that Laurie is too confused at the moment to think straight, and the children not old enough. Don't do anything rash. You're very vulnerable, dear girl, because you have a tender heart that makes it hard for you to say no, but sometimes it has to be said, or somebody might get terminally hurt.' He looked at her intently across the table. The soft lamplight emphasised the lean, rugged lines of his face, the square chin, the well-shaped mouth set in a straight line, and the dark pools of his eyes. 'Remember that you've got your own life to lead too.' He put a hand under her chin and tilted her head back, leaned across and kissed her swiftly on the lips.

'I will.' She trembled all over at his touch and the pressure of his lips on hers.

'Good,' he said, suddenly brisk. 'Now, do you want more coffee?'

'No.' She shook her head.

'Then let's get out of here,' he said softly, meaning-fully. 'Let's go home where we can be alone.'

He signalled for the bill, and a short while later they were driving away from Abbots through the mild night air, through country lanes lit by the pale light of the young moon.

They were silent for a while, each busy with their thoughts, each burningly aware of the other as they sat side by side in the dark car, and the vibes pulsated between them.

Imogen had never experienced anything like it before. Her whole being seemed alive and tingling in expectation. She longed to touch him, but found that she couldn't be quite that bold. As if sensing her desire, Daniel put out his left hand and touched her knee. 'All right?' he asked quietly.

'Fine, thank you, it's just that. . .' Her voice faltered and failed.

'It's rather overwhelming, isn't it? Being bowled over like this? Something extraordinary has happened to us, Imogen; we've fallen in love. It takes some getting used to. I didn't think it would happen to me at thirty-four. I planned to meet the right woman, get to know her over a sensible period of time, and then ask her to marry me. I didn't expect to meet by acci-dent an intelligent, chestnut-haired beauty with violet-blue eyes and a gentle heart, who would turn my own heart and mind upside-down in a few weeks.'

'Do you really feel like that about me?' she asked shyly.

'Yes, Imogen, I do,' he said firmly. Then added lightly, 'Thank God you bumped into me with your trolley, or I might still be waiting for the mythical right woman to come along!'

'Oh, but we would still have met next time you

visited Aunt Sophie,' she pointed out.

'Hush, woman!' interjected Daniel with mock severity. 'Don't spoil the fairy-tale.'

Breathlessly she asked, 'Are you sure that I am the right woman?'

'Oh, yes, absolutely, without a doubt. It's fate or something. I'm not normally given to reaching hasty conclusions about anything. I am a man of logic and I like to think my way through things, but this is different. . .we can't fight it, we belong together, don't you agree?' His deep voice was deeper than ever and thick with emotion. He turned his head briefly and in the shadowy moonlight she could see that he was smiling at her with great tenderness.

'Yes,' she said simply after a moment. There really wasn't anything else to say. For weeks she had known that there was something special between them, only she hadn't realised that he had known it too. She had thought it all on her side. Now he was admitting that it hadn't been like that at all, that he'd fallen in love with her at their first accidental meeting.

They were nearly home. A warm, intense but not uncomfortable silence hung between them, until Daniel said huskily, 'Am I rushing you, Imogen? I don't want to do anything to frighten you, but I want to make love to you.'

'No, Daniel, you're not rushing me, and I'm not frightened, not with you. And I want to make love to you too.' She felt bold enough now to put up a hand and touch his cheek with her fingertips.

He caught her hand and held it to his lips for a moment. 'I love you,' he murmured. 'And I've never said that to a woman before.' He glanced quickly at her. 'Oh, I don't mean that I've led an entirely blameless or celibate existence, but I have never pretended to be in love with anyone, ever. Does that surprise you?'

'Yes, it does,' she said. A vision sprang into her mind of Daniel standing with his arm round Sue Forsythe, and looking so close to her. Surely he had at least thought himself in love with Sue? She didn't want him to pretend otherwise, now that he had acknowledged that he was in love with her. The life he had led before she had met him, was his own affair. She could live with that, love affairs and all.

'Nevertheless,' he said, 'it's true. I've had affairs, but I've never pretended they were anything more than that. There was Sue. . .but you know all about that.' Imogen's heart jumped. She really was his first true love! Surely he wouldn't say that if it were not true? She gave him a tremulous smile. He touched her knee again. 'And what about you, my darling, have you been in love before?'

'No,' she replied with a little laugh. 'Though I sometimes thought I was.'

'Ah.'

They reached the outskirts of Steynhurst and he concentrated on negotiating the busy roundabout before turning the car into the top of the High Street and heading for the square.

Cleeves, Daniel's house, was tucked away down a short bush-lined drive just behind the health centre in the far corner of the square. The garden, especially at night with the health centre closed, was very secluded. Imogen was glad about this. The gossips would have had a field-day talking about the doctor and the twilight nurse returning from an evening out.

The house, except for a porch light, was in darkness.

Daniel unfastened his seat-belt. 'Coming home to a large empty house is a lonely business,' he said softly. 'It's nice to have company, especially your company.'

'I thought your parents were staying with you?'

'They moved out a couple of days ago to their bunga-low. We have the place to ourselves.'

'Oh.' Her heart thumped, her fingers seemed not to belong to her. She fumbled with her seat-belt, but it was Daniel who snapped it undone.

'Stay there,' he commanded as he got out and came round to the passenger side to open her door. He held out his hand and she rested hers on it as she stepped down from the car. 'Welcome to Cleeves,' he said. He bent and kissed her on the cheek. 'My home,' he added, 'is your home.'

'Oh, Daniel.' He put an arm round her shoulders. She looked up at him. 'It's all happening so fast.'

'I know, love, I feel it too, but I think we should trust to our instincts. And I've never felt so sure of mine in my life, have you?'

'No.'

He took her arm and guided her to the front door, which he then unlocked. He touched a switch just inside the door, and the hall flooded with amber light.

'Through here,' he said, taking her hand and leading her to a large room off the hall. He switched on more lights, soft, rose-coloured. 'The sitting-room.' He pushed her gently down on to a large, chintz-covered sofa. 'Coffee,' he asked, 'or something stronger?'

'I don't want anything, thank you,' she said rather primly, feeling suddenly shy.

'Nor I,' he said. His eyes met and held hers. He dropped to his knees beside her and wrapped his arms round her. 'Imogen,' he said huskily, 'I want you very much.'

'And I want you,' she whispered. Her body felt warm and heavy and throbbed with longing. She wanted to feel him touching her bare flesh.

He rained kisses on her face and neck, and his hands slipped beneath the sheer silk of her blouse and closed over her small, soft breasts. He stroked them, and her nipples rose, grew rigid. He unfastened her blouse and, with little licking kisses, caressed her naked breasts, his tongue and his lovely mobile mouth trailing sensuously over them. She gasped with pleasure and nuzzled the back of his neck.

Daniel raised his head and his large, clear hazel eyes met hers. 'I love you,' he breathed.

'I love you too.' She gazed back at him, her eyes huge and dark with desire.

For a moment he pulled away from her body.

'Will you marry me and soon?' he said simply. 'I mean for love, not for lust—though there will be plenty of that as well, I hope.'

'Oh, Daniel. . .yes, yes, I will marry you!'

He drew her to her feet. 'Let's go upstairs.' His hands caressed her small waist and neat, rounded buttocks as he guided her up the stairs before him. He led her into a lofty, typically Edwardian bedroom and switched on the bedside lamp beside a large bed. 'My room,' he said. 'And no one has ever shared it with me, Imogen.' He drew her into his arms and lowered his mouth to hers. She moulded herself to him, limp with longing. His tongue gently probed against her closed lips, teasing them open. Sure fingers unfastened the zip of her figure-hugging trousers, and with gentle fingers eased them down over her slender hips, until just the scrap of her lace panties lay between them. Very gently he pushed her down on to the bed and swung her leg up so that she was lying full-length. Reverently he covered her with the duvet.

'I'm sorry, my darling,' he said raggedly. 'I must get something. Not very romantic, but important. Don't move, I won't be a minute.' He straightened up and crossed to a door leading into a bathroom.

Imogen closed her eyes, and took a few deep breaths. She couldn't believe that this was happening to her, that she was allowing it to happen. Her heart and pulses were leaping, her loins taut, her vulva moist with longing.

Within a few moments he was back. Imogen opened her eyes and watched him coming towards her. He had removed his jacket and tie and was stripping off his shirt as he approached, and he shrugged it off and dropped it on a chair, and then did the same with his trousers. He stood there naked except for a pair of briefs, which did nothing to hide his arousal. His eyes holding hers, he slipped off his briefs and stood magnificently and totally nude before her. He was splendidly lean, yet well muscled, with a mat of fine black curly hairs covering his chest and arrowing down to his flat abdomen.

Imogen stared at him. 'You're beautiful,' she whispered.

'Hey,' he said with a lopsided smile, 'that's my line.'

He pulled back the duvet and stood looking down at her, then knelt on the bed. He dropped featherlight kisses on her forehead, her nose, her lips and her breasts. Slowly, with one hand he removed the lacy scrap of her panties. He bent and kissed the triangle of soft, downy hair. The pupils of his eyes were enormous, glittering. He shifted his position and knelt over her, his tanned, muscled legs gleaming in the lamplight, easily straddling her slim hips. 'Imogen!' He lowered his face to hers and their mouths met hungrily. He straightened himself out as they kissed, so that their bodies were lying touching from head to toe, his hardness against her softness as they melded into each other. The world, the room receded, became a blur. Nothing mattered but the two of them and their trembling, hot bodies, bound together, about to become as one.

The phone by the bed shrilled insistently.

Daniel raised his head and groaned. 'I don't believe it,' he said savagely.

Imogen, heart fluttering wildly, hating to feel him moving from her, muttered, 'Leave it; you're not on call.'

'I can't, my love, not at this time of night. It's my unlisted line, so it could be my parents, or one of my partners with something urgent—they wouldn't phone otherwise.'

His voice was strained, his face, his whole body was taut with frustration as he picked up the receiver. Imogen could vaguely hear a woman's voice at the other end. She moaned and turned her face into the pillow. Please God, don't let it be anything that will spoil all this, she thought.

Daniel said yes and no several times, and then he asked, 'What time was this?' and added, 'We'll go right away,' before replacing the receiver.

Imogen felt a coldness in the pit of her stomach. What had he meant when he had said 'We'll go right away'? She was suddenly alert. It must be Aunt Sophie. . .something must have happened to her.

Daniel turned to face her. 'Imogen,' he said evenly, 'that was Felicity, who is on call for me. She's just admitted Jason to hospital with a suspected appendicitis. Your aunt told her that I was with you.'

'Jason. . .oh, no,' she wailed softly. For a moment she lay there staring at him as the magic of being in his arms drained away. She was stunned by the news, and then she was rolling off the bed and grabbing at her clothes, dragging them on. 'Daniel, I must go to him now. Poor little Jason, and Laurie, poor Laurie, he will be in a dreadful state. . .they both need me, I must go to them at once.'

'My dear girl, of course you must. We will both go.' He was at once sure and authoritative. He heaved himself off the bed and disappeared into the bathroom, to emerge moments later in a turtle-neck sweater and cord trousers and trainers. 'Emergency gear,' he said, deliberately practical to break the spell of what had been between them. 'Always kept at the ready for night calls.'

Imogen was hugging her cashmere shawl round her shoulders. She was shivering. Daniel put his arms round her and held her tightly. 'You're in shock,' he said softly, 'what with one thing and another.' He kissed her forehead. 'You must be brave, love; your family will need you to be your usual calm self. Remember, I'm with you all the way.' He released her. 'Come on, let's get going to St Richard's and see what's happening to young Jason.'

He continued to reassure her as they drove to the hospital, telling her off gently but firmly when she suggested that she might have realised that the boy was not well had she been at home.

'That's nonsense, Imogen, and you know it. Felicity was called in to see him by Laurie directly he experienced severe pain and vomited. You couldn't have done more.'

'I might have noticed that he was off-colour earlier.'

'Rubbish. Stop blaming yourself—an inflamed appendix is an inflamed appendix. . .it can blow up quite suddenly and symptoms can be virtually non-existent until it happens.'

At the hospital they were told that Jason had been

referred to Theatre for surgery direct from the accident and emergency department, but they could wait in the paediatric unit to which he would be moved once he had recovered from his operation.

In the waiting area of the unit they found Laurie, sitting looking anxious, apprehensive and angry.

'I've been waiting for ages,' he said irritably when he saw them. 'And they still can't or won't tell me anything, except that he is having an appendicectomy.'

'They can't tell you anything until they have finished operating,' said Daniel kindly. 'Imogen will confirm that.'

'Oh, I've been told that already, I don't doubt it, but I could have done with some support earlier. Where on earth have you been, Imogen, and why didn't you let us know where you were going? I thought Mother knew, but she didn't.'

Imogen felt guilty, though she knew that she shouldn't do. Laurie was only accusing her because he was shocked and anxious. Of course it hadn't occurred to her that anything untoward could happen while she was out—why should it? And anyway, she hadn't known where Daniel was taking her.

Daniel said sharply, 'Laurie, we know that you are under a strain, but don't even think of blaming Imogen for what's happened, or for your not being able to get in touch with her. She doesn't have to have your permission to go out whenever and to wherever she pleases.'

The two men glared at each other, and then Laurie lowered his eyes. 'No,' he said sadly, 'I haven't the right to expect anything of her; I just hoped that she cared about us enough, that's all.' He sounded absolutely pathetic and defeated. Imogen felt terribly sorry for him.

'Laurie, of course I care, you know that, but I can't stay at home all the time just in case something happens. Nobody could do that, not even a loving wife and mother.'

An expression of intense pain passed over Laurie's face. 'You don't have to remind me,' he said fiercely, 'that I haven't got a loving wife at the moment, and you're the nearest thing to a mother that my children have just now.'

'Oh, Laurie, I'm so sorry I said that; I didn't mean to hurt you. It was clumsy of me.' She kissed him on the cheek. 'It was just that I——'

Daniel interrupted. 'Look,' he said in a calm voice, 'you're both upset by what's happened, you're both super-sensitive and neither of you wants to hurt the other.' He placed a hand on Laurie's shoulder. 'We'll have news soon, old chap, and if it's a simple appendicectomy, as it seems likely to be, Jason will be on the mend in a few days.'

His professional but friendly manner had some effect. Laurie calmed down. 'Yes, you're right,' he said, 'I went a bit over the top.' He turned to Imogen. 'Sorry I reacted that way. I know you are the last person in the world to hurt anyone.'

Before Imogen could reply, a green theatre-gowned figure appeared in the doorway, and Laurie rose from his chair and went forward to meet him. 'My son, Jason, is he all right?' he asked anxiously.

'Jason's fine, Mr Jackson; we've finished operating on him and he's in the recovery unit, but he'll be on his way here in a short while. Everything was quite straightforward. We've removed his appendix, which was very inflamed, and there were no complicating factors.'

'Thank God for that. Will I be able to see him?'

'For a few minutes when he returns to the ward, but, though he will be conscious, he will be very tired and need to sleep, and I suggest that you go home and do the same. Now I must go, there's another emergency to deal with.' He gave the three of them a wry smile. 'The lot of a registrar is pretty hectic. I only started working here this morning and I haven't seen my bed yet. Goodnight.' He turned on his heel and disappeared down the corridor.

'I thought you might have had a word with him,' said Laurie to Daniel, 'and got a bit more out of him, as you're Jason's GP.'

'Believe me, Laurie, there was no point. He couldn't tell me any more than he told you. If it had been someone I knew it might have been a different matter and we'd have had a friendly rather than a professional chat, but it would only have confirmed what you've been told.'

'Is that honestly true?' He sounded disbelieving.

'Honestly, no one's keeping anything back from you—there's nothing to keep back. The operation was successful, and there's no reason why his recovery shouldn't be just as straightforward, so stop worrying, Laurie.'

In the early hours of the morning they left the hospital, having seen Jason comfortably installed in the children's ward.

Daniel drove them back from St Richard's in Wichester to Steynhurst, through almost empty streets and deserted countryside. They were all silent on the trip home, each deep in their own thoughts. To Imogen, it seemed a lifetime away from the journey that she and Daniel had made hours before when they had driven, on a high of excitement and anticipation, back from their dinner at Abbots.

What had happened after that between them, the ecstatic lovemaking, the murmured endearments, seemed dreamlike, insubstantial in the face of the reality of Jason's medical emergency. Now he, Laurie, Patti and Aunt Sophie seemed the only important factors. It wasn't that her feelings for Daniel had changed but, almost against her will, they had paled to insignificance compared with the combined needs of the Jackson family. Daniel might be—in fact had said that he was—in love with her, but he didn't *need* her, the way that they did.

They drew up outside Aunt Sophie's house and Laurie, who had been sitting in the back of the car, got out, and said rather stiffly, 'Thanks for bringing us home, Daniel, and thank you for reassuring me; it was a great help.' He opened the front passenger door. 'Come on, Imogen, let's go and tell Mother the news.'

Imogen unfastened her seat-belt, but Daniel laid a hand on hers and spoke to Laurie. 'You go on in,' he said firmly. 'Imogen will be in shortly. I want a word with her.'

Laurie looked surprised and muttered huffily, 'Really? Oh, well, in that case I'll say goodnight.' He marched away, leaving the car door open.

'Are you going to call Kim now?' Imogen called after him.

Laurie hesitated. 'No,' he said sharply. 'I don't know. . .maybe tomorrow. . .' He stamped on into the house.

Imogen pulled the door to. Her heart ached for him; he looked so despondent, and she hated to see him behave badly in front of Daniel. 'He's still in shock,' she explained defensively. 'He wouldn't normally behave like this.'

'Of course he wouldn't. I quite understand, he's had a long hard night, but so have we, my darling. It could hardly have been more frustrating, could it?' He cupped her face with his hands and looked deep into her eyes. 'My dear, lovely Imogen, I'm so sorry the evening had to end as it did. I wanted to go on loving you all night; I wanted to prove my love for you.'

Imogen said softly, returning his gaze, every fibre of her being longing to be in his arms, 'I think you did, in an entirely practical way, taking me to the hospital, staying with Laurie and me, being so patient.'

'Anyone would have done that.'

She shook her head. 'No, they wouldn't. For some men, love stops with sex; they think one equates with the other, and they wouldn't be so understanding about dependent friends or relations. You're remarkably kind and sensitive, Daniel. Go on being that whatever happens.'

'Whatever happens! Sounds ominous. What do you mean, Imogen?'

'Nothing specific,' she said hurriedly, not being sure herself why the phrase had popped into her head.

Daniel frowned. 'You're apprehensive. There's no need, you know, and no earthly reason why Jason's emergency appendicectomy should make any difference to us. Of course, hospital visiting and supporting the family will be time-consuming for a bit, but fundamentally there will be no difference. In fact we might even see more of each other, as I shall be at your disposal when off duty, if you need me—remember that.' His voice was gentle and understanding.

'Oh, I will, thank you,' she said in a tattered sort of voice. He was so kind. He was everything a woman could want. A real gentleman. Her eyes misted with tears.

He kissed her eyelids and then her lips very softly, and cradled her head against his chest for a moment. 'There, love,' he murmured, 'I mustn't keep you up any longer; you need your bed. Thank you for everything earlier, it was wonderful. We'll soon pick up from where we left off.'

'Will we?' Suddenly she was full of doubt. It didn't seem possible that they could ever recapture the magic of those moments before that shattering telephone call. Life wasn't like that; you didn't often get a second chance. Laurie had been right about her commitment to the family—they needed her to care for them, and that was why she had come to Steynhurst. Her clear mind might tell her that she was entitled to a life of her own, but her generous heart doubted it. Jason's sudden illness was just a reminder to her of where her duty lay.

She shivered with a kind of primitive foreboding as Daniel came round to open the door for her. What did the future hold for her and for him?

He helped her from the car, brought her hands to his lips and kissed her fingertips gently. 'Goodnight, love, sleep well, and don't worry, *all will be well*, I promise.' His gleaming hazel eyes looked down at her with love and compassion for a moment, and then he released her hands, got back into the car and drove off.

Imogen shivered again. 'I wonder,' she whispered as she mounted the steps to the side-door.

CHAPTER TEN

DANIEL's words, 'all will be well', which he'd spoken with such confidence, kept going round in her head when, after having reassured Aunt Sophie and a tearful Patti that Jason was out of danger, Imogen eventually retired to her room. She wished she felt as confident as he about their future, but she couldn't shake off the feeling of foreboding that Jason's emergency had triggered.

It was ridiculous, but a fact. She felt guilty because she and Daniel had been making love when Jason was taken ill. Common sense told her that it wouldn't have made the slightest difference what she was doing at that time—the outcome would have been the same—but that did nothing to diminish her feeling of guilt.

If, her silly thoughts suggested, she hadn't started this twilight nursing job, which Laurie so hated her doing, she wouldn't have been out with Daniel that night. And if, her muddled mind rambled on, she hadn't been out, she would have been at home to help Jason when he came back from the party feeling ill. And a fat lot of use that would have been, she told herself again, for the outcome would have been exactly the same. Try as she might, she couldn't make sense out of her thoughts, which kept going round and round in circles.

That she and Daniel were in love was indisputable. The fact that they were only just getting to know each other didn't matter a jot. She had accepted his proposal. Had agreed to marry him soon. But how could she rush into marriage now? Surely Daniel would understand when she explained how she felt more than ever committed to Aunt Sophie and the others, and would agree to wait? They could get engaged, which would put their relationship on a firm footing. In fact, an engagement period would be a wonderfully tender time of getting to know each other. They would be acknowledged as a pair, but she would be free to carry on looking after the Jacksons until their future was more secure and they were less vulnerable.

In spite of having little sleep, Imogen was up and dressed early, but when she went down to the kitchen it was to find Laurie, looking haggard and drawn and unshaven, already there.

'I've just rung the hospital,' he said. 'I know it's early but I couldn't wait any longer. They said that Jason's had a comfortable night, whatever that means.'

'Exactly that, I should think,' said Imogen gently. 'It was a very straightforward operation because it was done in good time. He would have been given pain-killers and sedation last night if needed. He's going to be a bit sore for a few days, but he should soon be on the mend. We'll have him back home in a week or so to convalesce, and in a short while he'll be quite his usual self.'

Laurie looked at her sadly. 'And will you still be around to help look after him, or are you going to abandon us and set up some sort of ménage with Daniel Granger?' he asked, managing to sound both pathetic and faintly sarcastic.

'Oh, Laurie, don't be so melodramatic. As if I would *abandon* you, as you put it. Don't worry, I'll be around for as long as you need me.'

'Is that a promise?'

'It is,' she said firmly, though aware that his idea of need and hers might differ considerably. 'Look, why don't you go up and get shaved while I make the tea?'

'OK, if I must.' Reluctantly, with dragging footsteps, he left the kitchen and she heard him making his way upstairs.

The phone rang as she switched on the kettle, and she guessed at once that it was Daniel, as nobody else would ring this early on a Sunday morning. Although she had seen him only a few hours before, the usual thrill of pleasure prickled through her and caught at her throat as she said huskily, 'Five-one-three-four-six-two.'

Daniel's familiar, deep rich voice spoke in her ear. 'Imogen—hello, love. Have you phoned the hospital yet about Jason?'

'Yes—got the usual jargon that he had a comfortable night.'

'Well, I'm sure that's true. There's no reason why he should have complications, though of course they can happen. But don't worry, love, he should make a speedy recovery.'

'That's what I've been telling Laurie, but he's frightfully shaken by what's happened—it's really thrown him. He's going to need a lot of support.'

There was a slight pause, then Daniel said softly and slowly, as if picking his words with care, 'Imogen, don't let that too tender heart of yours get carried away. Do what you must for your Aunt Sophie and the rest of the family, but remember that you have your own life to lead. You owe yourself and me something too. I need you and you need me. This was crystal-clear last night. I want to give you love in return for your love. You must learn to take a little as well as give. Don't you agree?'

She hesitated. 'Yes—of course.'

'You don't sound very certain.'

'Don't I?'

'No, my dear, you don't.' His voice held a tinge of bitterness. 'Are you by any chance having second thoughts about marrying me?'

She was shocked by the suggestion. 'Oh, Daniel, no, of course not. I love you. I want to marry you, but. . .'

'But. . .?'

Imogen felt her mouth go dry as she drew in a ragged breath. This wasn't what she had expected. It was ironic that he had immediately brought up the very subject that she had wanted to speak about in a more leisurely, persuasive fashion. She found her voice, and said quietly, 'I need time. Aunt Sophie and the others need me. I thought we would get engaged for a few months, and perhaps get married in the autumn, or early next year.'

'*No*, my dear Imogen,' he said firmly, almost explosively. 'No *way* do I want to wait that long. What a pointless exercise, now that we have made up our minds. I suggest that we get officially engaged within the next few days, and plan for a June wedding, with all the trimmings if you wish—bridesmaids, the lot. I'm sure we're capable of organising that. I want the privilege of caring for you, loving you, and letting the world see that I love you as soon as possible, not at some vague future date. I can be patient, but not that patient. Surely you want that too, for us to be together all the time?'

'Of course I do,' she said, trying to make her voice as firm as his, though she was full of trepidation, as he sounded so fierce. She must say what she had to. She gathered all her courage together and continued, 'But I *do* have a commitment to the Jackson family.

I won't abandon them at the snap of your fingers, however much I may want to be your wife. Surely you understand that?'

'I agree that you have had obligations but I think you have fulfilled them, or will have done within a few weeks. Jason should make a straightforward recovery, your aunt is getting increasingly mobile and independent, and you have extra help in the shop. So tell me, Imogen, if the problem of your commitments to your godmother and her family were resolved, would you marry me in June?'

She said without hesitation, 'I would marry you tomorrow, Daniel.'

'I'm glad to hear it,' he said drily. 'Right, that's all I wanted to know. We'll work something out, leave it to me. But a June wedding it's going to be. Now I must away; I've a couple of calls to do before surgery. Goodbye, love, I expect I'll see you some time later.' He was suddenly very brisk and efficient, and his goodbye was clipped and almost impersonal in spite of the endearment.

His receiver went down and she said, 'Goodbye, Daniel,' to an empty phone. She thought wryly, That always seems to be happening to me. He hadn't exactly sounded cross, just businesslike. Not that she'd blame him if he were cross, as he had every right to be angry with her for seeming to care more for Aunt Sophie and the family than she did for him.

Nothing, of course, could have been further from the truth—she loved him with every fibre of her being, sexually, spiritually, emotionally, and surely he must know that! The vibes had been there between them from the very beginning, pulling them closer and closer without words being necessary. She longed to have him repeat the passionate lovemaking they had begun the previous night, this time without interruption. She knew he would bring her to an ecstatic climax as he had been so near to doing. Her body thrilled at the thought of this intimate contact, body to body.

There was a clatter of feet on the stairs, and Patti appeared. Slowly Imogen replaced the receiver on the hook and took command of her wayward thoughts.

'Dad says Jason's going to be fine,' Patti blurted out. 'When can I go and see him?'

'Not until this afternoon,' Imogen replied firmly. 'He needs to rest.'

'Will he have a big scar?' Patti wanted to know.

'Only a small one, I should think.'

'Oh.' Patti seemed disappointed. 'I thought it might be ginormous.'

'Don't be so ghoulish.'

'What's ghoulish?'

'Well, roughly speaking, feeding off someone's misfortune. In this case, poor Jason's scar. I'm sure he doesn't want a big one.'

'Oh, I don't know, he'll want to show it off at school, especially to Jane Thompson, so the bigger the better,' said Patti with a giggle. Then she stopped giggling abruptly, frowned, and asked anxiously, 'But he is going to be all right, isn't he, Imogen? He's. . .he's not going to die?'

'No, love, he's not going to die,' replied Imogen, giving her a hug. 'Though he'll be a bit quiet for a day or two, and won't be quite himself, but that's quite normal after an operation.'

Imogen was glad that she had warned Patti not to expect too much from Jason when they visited that afternoon. He looked small and pathetic, attached to a fluid drip, with a 'Nil by Mouth' notice above his bed. He was, she noticed with a practised eye, a little flushed, and she saw by his chart that he was running a slight temperature.

'Nothing to worry about,' assured a smiling staff nurse who came to speak to them. She moistened Jason's lips with a gauze swab dipped in water. 'He's on antibiotics, and it'll soon go down.'

They didn't stay long, for although he was pleased to see them he tired quickly, and his eyelids began to droop as they left his bedside with promises to return the following day.

In spite of the nurse's assurance, both Laurie and Patti were still terribly anxious about him, and Imogen had to do a lot of reassuring of her own as they drove home.

On Monday morning she was in the middle of massaging her godmother's oedematous legs prior to putting on her support stockings, when that lady said quietly, 'You're very thoughtful today, Imogen; is anything wrong? You seem preoccupied.'

For a moment Imogen was tempted to pour out all her troubles. Then she realised that she couldn't. How could she explain that part of her problem was Aunt Sophie herself, and the emotional hold she unwittingly had over her god-daughter? It would be too cruel. She would feel dreadful if she thought that she was standing in the way of Imogen's happiness.

She prevaricated, and told a half-truth. 'I was thinking about Laurie and the children and how much they need their mother.'

'Really?' said Aunt Sophie, sounding sceptical, and it was clear that she only half believed her. 'I thought it might be something more personal than that.'

Imogen shook her head and told another little white lie. 'No,' she said, 'nothing personal. I just wish that Laurie would get in touch with Kim. Tell her that

Jason has had an op and that he and Patti need her, even if he won't admit to needing her himself.'

Aunt Sophie said sadly, 'That's what I have been trying to tell him, but he's adamant. His pride's badly hurt, Imogen, and he won't admit how much he's missing her. Yet I know she would come like a shot if he asked her to.'

'She wouldn't before, so what makes you think that she will now if he asks?'

'I've had a letter from her, begging me to get Laurie to ask her to return to him. Fortunately it came when both you and Daniel were out, and Pam brought it up.'

'She's written, and he still won't ask her! I can't believe it of him.'

'She made it a condition that I didn't tell him she'd written; just wanted me to persuade him to seek her out.'

'So she has her pride too, and that puts you in an intolerable position.'

'Doesn't it just! I want to respect both their feelings, but I also want to do what's best for the children, and that would be to bring them together as soon as possible. I'm sure they still love each other.'

'So am I,' said Imogen, 'and isn't love supposed to conquer all things, including pride? Aunt Sophie, you must do everything you can to bring about a reconciliation.'

'That's my intention,' said her aunt. 'What I need is someone to advise me who can look at the situation dispassionately and intelligently, and do you know, I think I know who may just fill that role?'

'Who?' asked Imogen.

'Daniel. Your Dr Granger, he's a clear thinker and the children's GP, and I've a feeling that he'll be pleased to help. I think he may have his own reasons for wanting the Jackson family sorted out, don't you, Imogen?' she said with a twinkle in her eye. It was a direct challenge.

Imogen, whose heart had lurched when Aunt Sophie had mentioned his name, went faintly red and said softly, 'You've guessed, haven't you, about Daniel and me? He proposed to me yesterday.'

'I'm not surprised. I hope you accepted. It wasn't very hard to work out, my dear, the way you feel about each other, as it's been quite clear for weeks to a keen and loving observer that there was something between you. It was one of the reasons that I was afraid for Laurie. I could see that he hadn't got a hope in hell with you once Daniel appeared on the scene, which is just as well, considering he's still, although he won't acknowledge it, in love with his wife.'

'Yes, if only they can be brought together, if they will just forget their silly pride. One of them just has to come round. So much depends on it.'

Aunt Sophie suddenly sounded quite confident. 'Oh, they will, Imogen, believe me, we'll get them together with Daniel's help. He's a very resourceful person, he'll think of something, especially with the added incentive of wanting you to himself as soon as possible.' She gave Imogen a smile. 'He's the sort of man who always does come up with a solution. He'll make a splendid husband, just right for you; he's strong and decisive, and you need a strong man to love and support you, my dear. You're sometimes too generous for your own good. Daniel will make you say no occasionally.'

At that moment her phone rang, and as Aunt Sophie picked it up and listened, her smile widening, 'Why, Daniel,' she said cheerfully, 'Imogen and I were just talking about you.'

Imogen, pulses racing, wondered what on earth he was phoning her godmother about.

There was a muffled comment from the other end of the phone and Aunt Sophie said on a laugh, 'No, I promise you it was all good.' And then more seriously she said, 'Yes, do come this afternoon. I very much want to see you.' Daniel then said something else, and Aunt Sophie replied, 'Yes, I'll explain to Imogen. Goodbye, Daniel, I'll see you later.'

She put down her phone, and sat for a moment in silence, thoughtfully regarding Imogen. Then she said, 'Daniel's been doing a lot of thinking about Laurie and Kim, apparently, since talking to you yesterday. He has an idea. He's coming to talk to me this afternoon, preferably without Laurie's knowledge. Can we get him off the premises for an hour or so?'

'Nothing could be simpler—he talked about going to the wholesalers today. If I help Doreen in the shop he can go off this afternoon.'

'Good, will you fix that, then, Imogen?'

'Will do.' Still curious, she asked, 'What else did Daniel say?'

'Nothing much. Just that he and I between us would persuade Kim to come home, but I don't know how he intends to do this. And it's no good speculating, my dear, as he'll tell us in his own good time. He sounded very sure of himself. He must love you very much, to be so determined to get my family sorted out and relieve you of any responsibility you might feel for us.'

'Yes,' she murmured. 'I believe he does.'

A few minutes later, her heart and mind still full of Daniel, she took herself down to the shop and suggested to Laurie that he go to the wholesalers that afternoon. Quite unsuspicious, he agreed with alacrity, saying that he would be glad of a distraction in between visiting Jason later in the morning and again that evening with Patti.

The shop was busy when Daniel appeared soon after lunch, and he waited just inside the door while Imogen dealt with a customer.

When she was free he crossed to the counter. Armed with his medical case, wearing a lightweight fawn suit, white shirt and colourful tie, he looked cool and professional as he approached. Her heart flipped. It was so good to see him, solid and reassuring.

'Hi, love,' he said softly, and smiled into her eyes. 'Is the coast clear. . .is it safe for me to go up and see your aunt?'

Imogen nodded. 'Yes,' she said in a whispery voice. 'I'll take you up.'

'No, there's no need; you're busy. . .I'll make my own way up.' He eased round the narrow space behind the counter and let himself out through the door that led to the domestic quarters, closing it firmly behind him.

As if, thought Imogen despondently, he wanted to make quite sure that I wouldn't follow him, wouldn't take part in his discussion with Aunt Sophie. Her mind seethed with questions. What was he proposing to Aunt Sophie, what plan was he putting forward to reconcile Laurie and Kim? Her godmother had said that he seemed so certain of success, but how could he be? What made him so sure? For some idiotic reason she felt that her whole future was being decided, and with a dull ache she felt that she had no say in the matter. It was a silly line of thought, but one that persisted.

She was glad when the shop got even busier and she had to concentrate on serving, for it took her mind off what was going on upstairs in the sitting-room.

It was about an hour later that Daniel reappeared in the doorway behind the counter. He caught Imogen's eye. 'Can Doreen manage if I steal you away for a little while?' he asked.

'I expect so,' she said rather breathlessly.

He nodded and turned away.

'Of course I can manage,' said Doreen, who was standing at the till and had overheard him. 'You go through and talk to the doctor. I do hope that Mrs Jackson is all right. . . he's been a long time with her.'

'I'm sure she's fine,' said Imogen, knowing that the reason for Daniel's visit had nothing to do with Aunt Sophie's physical well-being and feeling slightly guilty at the deception, 'but I'd better go and see what he wants.'

Mind racing, heart pumping painfully, she stepped through into the dim corridor behind the shop. What would Daniel have to say to her. . .would it be good news or bad, or nothing concrete at all? And how would his news affect their future? Would he be pleased or angry? Endless questions whirled through her mind.

He was standing in the doorway of the kitchen at the end of the corridor. His face was in shadow, so she could get no clue as to his feelings from his expression.

'I—I thought we were going up to see Aunt Sophie,' she stammered.

'We will, all in good time. Come here, my darling Imogen,' he said in a commanding but husky voice. 'I've some wonderful news to share with you.'

He held out his arms, and she moved slowly, almost like an automaton, down the corridor into them. He held her close to him for a moment or two in silence, and she could hear his heart thumping rhythmically, in long, steady beats in his broad chest.

He kissed the top of her head, and nuzzled the back of her neck. His breath was warm and sweet on her skin. 'So soft,' he murmured, 'so delightful, so beautiful and so nearly mine at last.'

He sounded like a romantic hero in an old-fashioned book, she thought as she looked up into his rugged face. His firm lips were parted in a half-smile, and his eyes were pools of bright hazel-green tenderness full of love. 'What news?' she whispered, putting up a hand and running a finger along the faint line of stubble on his square jaw. 'Tell me.'

'The best news in the world. Kim's coming home on the first available flight. Your godmother and I have had a long talk with her on the phone. She's pocketing her pride and is going to ask Laurie to take her back. She's longing to see her children, and him.'

Imogen let out a long, trembling sigh. 'Oh, Daniel, how wonderful. How did you manage to persuade her?'

'It wasn't too difficult. After all, we knew from her letter that she wanted a reconciliation. I pointed out that, as the children's doctor, I knew that they were pining for her, and I was concerned for their health, and that they would never be quite normal without her. I rather played up Jason's emergency, though reassuring her that he was out of immediate danger— and implied that Laurie was so distraught over it that he couldn't face phoning her in person, to tell her how much she was needed. I rather took advantage of the situation and let her into my secret about being abandoned as a child and knowing what it felt like. A bit melodramatic, a bit of a tear-jerker, but it worked. She's phoning Laurie later to give him the news.'

'Oh, my darling, I'm so very pleased. . .thank you,

thank you.' Trembling, she reached up and kissed him softly, yet with a restrained passion, full on his firm mouth.

His eyebrows quirked up in surprise. 'Such an extravagant thank-you—what for, my love?'

'For working a miracle, bringing Kim and Laurie together, giving the twins back their mother, and making things all right for us. You deserve a big thank-you for all that, darling Daniel.' She kissed her fingertips and pressed them against his lips. 'But I daren't kiss you again, not properly, not as I'd like to, or I won't be able to stop.'

'Then don't stop, my dearest love. I won't object, you know that.' His hazel eyes, very green, twinkled down at her.

She shook her head. 'We'll only be interrupted, and I couldn't bear that. Laurie will be back with Patti any minute, since he's collecting her from school on his way from the wholesalers.'

Daniel caught her hand in his, and kissed her palm. 'You've called me darling several times in a few minutes,' he said softly, his eyes gleaming. 'I like to hear it. You don't do it often enough.'

'I've felt rather shy about saying it until now.'

'Oh, my precious love, you must never feel shy with me, not about anything. We must be free, and open and honest with each other in every way, mind and body.' He blew on her fringe of bright chestnut hair and trailed a kiss across her forehead with lips and tongue. She shivered with pleasure and closed her eyes, and he dropped featherlight kisses on her closed lids. 'Promise me that.'

She opened her violet-blue eyes and met his hazel-green ones in a long, loving exchange.

'I promise,' she whispered.

'And promise that you'll marry me in June, now that Kim is coming home!'

'I promise.'

'Good, that's what I wanted to hear. Now let's go up and see your godmother—she's bursting to discuss Kim's return with you.'

Slowly, their arms still twined around each other, they went up the stairs to the sitting-room, where Aunt Sophie sat in her favourite chair at the far window.

'Would I be right,' she said with a beaming smile as they approached her, 'in thinking that I'll soon be regaining a daughter-in-law but losing a god-daughter?'

Imogen went forward and dropped a kiss on her godmother's cheek. 'Not losing a god-daughter, Aunt Sophie—you'll never lose me, not even when I marry Daniel.'

'And when's that going to be?'

'Next month, in June. Now that everything's going to be taken care of here, we thought the sooner the better.'

'Quite right too; no sense in hanging around, life's too short—make the most of every minute.' They were both standing by her chair and she caught their hands in hers. 'I'm so happy for you both,' she said softly. 'You deserve a wonderful life together. Make every moment count. Love each other, respect and honour each other.' Her eyes misted over. 'A June wedding,' she murmured. 'It's just perfect, a perfect month to be married in. I was married on June the twenty-fourth, Midsummers Day.'

Imogen and Daniel smiled at each other and nodded, understanding without words.

'We're going to be married on Midsummers Day,' said Imogen softly, keeping her fingers crossed and praying that the church would be free on that day. 'We've just decided.'

It seemed to be a time for miracles, for Midsummers Day fell at midweek, and the church was free.

My wedding-day, thought Imogen as she woke early to a glorious blue and gold midsummer morning five weeks later. It didn't seem possible, but it had come at last, the day she was to marry Daniel. He would look stunning in formal grey tails which would complement his broad shoulders and lean hips, she thought, picturing him vividly, coolly elegant and commanding as he waited for her to join him at the altar in the parish church.

A great rush of love washed over her at the thought of spending the rest of her life with him. His future was her future, the past was past. He was her sole commitment, now that Kim was here to look after Aunt Sophie and the family, and she would devote her life to making him happy.

She looked round her small but pretty bedroom with the chintzy curtains and bedcovering affectionately. It had been her own room whenever she had visited. It was the room to which she had returned a few months ago when she came home to look after Aunt Sophie. Now it would no longer be hers, for her home was with Daniel.

The thought of sharing Cleeves with him thrilled her. It was a lovely house, a family house, a place that she hoped they would fill with children, making it a home. They had both agreed, during one of their all too few intimate meetings over the last five hectic weeks, that they wanted a large family. They both loved children, and had even discussed the possibility of fostering, in addition to having their own family, starting of course with little Jonathan Butterworth, who held a special place in both their hearts.

'We'll share our abundance of love with those who need it most,' Daniel had said one evening when they had a few minutes to themselves, 'and bring the sort of happiness that we have into their young lives.'

Readily Imogen had agreed, reflecting that with few words they seemed to be in complete accord on the important matters of everyday life and living. They were both used to loving and giving, it seemed only right that once they were married they would continue to give happiness to others. Daniel had teased her about her generous heart, but his, she knew, was equally generous.

What a wonderful start to a marriage, thought Imogen now as she slid out of bed and crossed to the open window that looked over the walled garden at the rear of the house, with everything in harmony. The garden was full of delphiniums and lupins, roses and sweet-peas, and their gentle scents drifted up to her as she leaned out of the window. It was a perfect day for a perfect marriage.

A few hours later they were married, and they emerged from the church to a barrage of photographers and a joyous pealing of bells.

'Happy?' murmured Daniel as he drew Imogen into his arms and kissed her rather formally at the request of the cameramen.

'Frighteningly, ecstatically, madly happy,' whispered Imogen, 'and you?'

'The same, my dearest love, the same.'

'I just wish,' said Imogen a little wistfully, 'that everyone could be as happy as we are.'

Daniel gave a rich, low laugh. 'Well, of course you do,' he said softly. 'It's your nature to want to share everything, even your love. I'm resigned to that. But, my darling, we've enough love for each other and to spare. Now will you come here and be kissed again properly, and this time just for me? Forget them.' He waved a hand towards the photographers.

'Yes, please,' she said simply as she went into his arms. She looked up at him and smiled. 'It's just like coming home,' she added quietly, almost reverently, as his arms enfolded her.

'Home, my darling, is where the heart is,' he said firmly, somehow managing not to sound sugary and sentimental, but simply warm and loving. 'And home, here in my heart, is where you belong.'

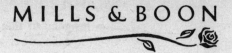

MILLS & BOON

OCTOBER 1995 HARDBACK TITLES

Romance

The Santa Sleuth *Heather Allison*	H4340	0 263 14489 5
A Devious Desire *Jacqueline Baird*	H4341	0 263 14490 9
Steamy December *Ann Charlton*	H4342	0 263 14491 7
Edge of Deception *Daphne Clair*	H4343	0 263 14492 5
Society Page *Ruth Jean Dale*	H4344	0 263 14493 3
Silver Bells *Val Daniels*	H4345	0 263 14494 1
Mistress for Hire *Angela Devine*	H4346	0 263 14495 X
An Irresistible Flirtation *Victoria Gordon*	H4347	0 263 14496 8
Hostage of Passion *Diana Hamilton*	H4348	0 263 14497 6
Dark Fever *Charlotte Lamb*	H4349	0 263 14498 4
The Price of Deceit *Cathy Williams*	H4350	0 263 14499 2
The Unlikely Santa *Leigh Michaels*	H4351	0 263 14500 X
Three Times a Bride *Catherine Spencer*	H4352	0 263 14501 8
Never Go Back *Anne Weale*	H4353	0 263 14502 6
Never a Stranger *Patricia Wilson*	H4354	0 263 14503 4
The Mermaid Wife *Rebecca Winters*	H4355	0 263 14504 2

LEGACY of LOVE

A Lady of Expectations *Stephanie Laurens*	M369	0 263 14583 2
Felon's Fancy *Sarah Westleigh*	M370	0 263 14584 0

LOVE ON CALL

A Voice in the Dark *Josie Metcalfe*	D287	0 263 14585 9
The Generous Heart *Margaret O'Neill*	D288	0 263 14586 7

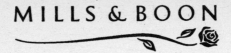

MILLS & BOON

OCTOBER 1995 LARGE PRINT TITLES

Romance

When Enemies Marry... *Lindsay Armstrong*	847	0 263 14315 5
Burning with Passion *Emma Darcy*	848	0 263 14316 3
Master of Seduction *Sarah Holland*	849	0 263 14317 1
Come Back Forever *Stephanie Howard*	850	0 263 14318 X
The Trusting Game *Penny Jordan*	851	0 263 14319 8
Deadly Rivals *Charlotte Lamb*	852	0 263 14320 1
Treacherous Longings *Anne Mather*	853	0 263 14321 X
Wanted: Wife and Mother *Barbara McMahon*	854	0 263 14322 8

LEGACY*of*LOVE

The Devil's Mark *Joanna Makepeace*	0 263 14427 5
The Absentee Earl *Clarice Peters*	0 263 14428 3

LOVE ON CALL

Practice Makes Marriage *Marion Lennox*	0 263 14337 6
Loving Remedy *Joanna Neil*	0 263 14338 4
Crisis Point *Grace Read*	0 263 14628 6
A Subtle Magic *Meredith Webber*	0 263 14629 4

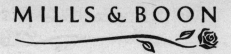

MILLS & BOON

NOVEMBER 1995 HARDBACK TITLES

Romance

LEGACY *of* LOVE

LOVE ON CALL

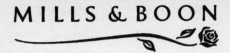

MILLS & BOON

NOVEMBER 1995 LARGE PRINT TITLES

Romance

Forgotten Husband *Helen Bianchin*	855	0 263 14355 4
Never a Bride *Diana Hamilton*	856	0 263 14356 2
Legally Binding *Jessica Hart*	857	0 263 14357 0
Emerald Fire *Sandra Marton*	858	0 263 14358 9
A Reluctant Attraction *Valerie Parv*	859	0 263 14359 7
The Ultimate Betrayal *Michelle Reid*	860	0 263 14360 0
Vengeful Seduction *Cathy Williams*	861	0 263 14361 9
Second-Best Bride *Sara Wood*	862	0 263 14362 7

LEGACY*of*LOVE

Ginnie Come Lately *Carola Dunn*	0 263 14429 1
Chevalier's Pawn *Sarah Westleigh*	0 263 14430 5

LOVE ON CALL

Taken for Granted *Caroline Anderson*	0 263 14513 1
Hell on Wheels *Josie Metcalfe*	0 263 14514 X
Laura's Nurse *Elisabeth Scott*	0 263 14630 8
Vet in Demand *Carol Wood*	0 263 14631 6